Madeleine St John was born in Sydney and was the first Australian woman to be shortlisted for the Man Booker Prize (in 1997 for her novel, *The Essence of the Thing*). She died in 2006.

Also by Madeleine St John

A Pure Clear Light

The Essence of the Thing

A Stairway to Paradise

The Women in Black

MADELEINE ST JOHN

ABACUS

ABACUS

This edition published in 2011 by Abacus
Reprinted 2013

First published by Abacus in 1994

First published in Great Britain in 1993 by André Deutsch
First published in Australia in 2009 by The Text Publishing Company

A CIP catalogue record for this book is available from the British Library.

ISBN: 978-0-349-12338-7

Typeset in Goudy by M Rules
Printed and bound in Great Britain by
Clays Ltd, St Ives plc

Papers used by Abacus are from well-managed forests and other responsible sources.

MIX
Paper from
responsible sources
FSC® C104740

Abacus
An imprint of
Little, Brown Book Group
100 Victoria Embankment
London EC4Y 0DY

An Hachette UK Company
www.hachette.co.uk

www.littlebrown.co.uk

This book is dedicated
To the memory of
M. & Mme. J. M. Cargher

Bruce Beresford

Madeleine and Me

Nineteen-sixty was my first year as an indifferent student at Sydney University. In pursuit of the prettiest girls I joined the Sydney University Players where I was an even more indifferent actor, easily outclassed by the stars of the era – who included John Bell, John Gaden, Germaine Greer, Arthur Dignam, Clive James and Robert Hughes.

Madeleine St John (she pronounced the name 'Synjin', though I understand her family preferred the standard 'Saint John') was to be found backstage, helping with the costumes and props. Definitely not one of the university's glamour girls, she still managed to be striking. Tiny and with rusty-red hair, she always reminded me of a sparrow with her darting movements, her beak-like nose, her inquisitive eyes. Her odd appearance contrived to prevent her performing in anything other than minor theatrical roles, although she was cast, rather mendaciously I thought, in a revue, *Dead Centre*, in which she appeared, singing, dancing and dressed in red crepe, as Lola Montez.

I can recall only a couple of conversations with her – all vague now (forty-eight years later!) – including one where she expressed a passion for the poetry of Thomas Hardy. I distinctly remember being so in awe of her wide reading— 'are you really unaware of the work of Gwen Raverat and Djuna Barnes?' – her forthrightness and her wit, that, in order to prevent my self-esteem plummeting, I took evasive action. The factor which distinguished her from virtually all of our contemporaries was that she was the daughter of a famous father, Edward St John, a prominent QC and Liberal politician, though if father or family was mentioned she immediately made it clear the subject was taboo.

I left for England in 1963 and lost track of Madeleine for thirty years. My attempts at establishing myself as a film director slowly met with some success. One day, in 1993, I was having lunch with Clive James, by now an internationally known critic and poet, when he mentioned that a novel he'd just read, *The Women in Black*, was by our old university colleague, Madeleine St John – and was a comic masterpiece. I bought a copy immediately, agreed with Clive's assessment, and called the publisher for Madeleine's number.

She was cordial and cheery over the phone, said she'd seen a number of my films over the years and was delighted I wanted to film her novel.

A few days later I went to see her. She was living in a large apartment on the top floor of a council house building in Notting Hill. The area had been derelict but was now being gentrified. Madeleine must have qualified for rent assistance some years previously and there was no indication that her financial situation had improved. The furnishing was basic, the most striking items being a number of well-thumbed paperbacks and a vicious white cat, which snarled and clawed the air whenever it considered I had approached too close to its mistress.

She seemed to have become even smaller, the rusty-red hair maintained its aura with bottled assistance and she was almost permanently attached to an oxygen tank with a long tube – the result of emphysema. She was as sharp-tongued as ever and tartly dismissed my query about whether it was advisable to smoke so heavily with such a condition. She was happy to talk at length about literature, classical music and jazz. Her opinions, as always, were firm and precise – contemporary novelists being airily dismissed as a bunch of parvenus. Mitsuko Uchida, she insisted, was the finest classical pianist and Art Tatum the greatest jazz pianist. Personal information was much harder to obtain, though I found out that she had married Chris Tillam, a fellow student from Sydney, in 1965. They had lived in San Francisco for a few years, where he studied film. Once his course was completed they decided to go to London. Madeleine went on ahead but 'he never arrived'. She made no further comments, so I gathered he had met another lady – and that was the end of the marriage.

She refused to discuss her Australian relatives, just as she had back at university, although she made vague references to their 'ill-treatment' of her. Subsequent meetings with a couple of charming members of her family, in Australia, have led me to believe that Madeleine never recovered, while still in high school, from the shock of the death, by suicide, of her mother. She then created a cast of evil relations who had accepted her father's re-marriage.

In the late 1960s, following her alleged abandonment by her husband, she lived around London in a number of apartments, sharing with various Australian university friends. To the astonishment of some she fell under the influence of a dubious Indian mystic, Swami Ji, and for a couple of years adopted Indian clothes and assumed an Indian name.

She supported herself with odd jobs, mostly in bookshops and an antique shop in the West End, although she tried to vary this routine by applying, at one point, and unsuccessfully, for a position as Kenneth Tynan's secretary. It was not until sometime in 1991 that Madeleine decided to write a book herself, convinced, she told me, she could do at least as well as the authors of so many of the books she was selling. She was fifty-two when *The Women in Black* was published in 1993 and it is the only one of her four novels to be set in Australia. It is difficult not to see Madeleine herself in the clever and sensitive young heroine, Lesley Miles, though the well observed lower middle-class family background she describes with such affection was certainly not her own, as she grew up in the smart suburb of Castlecrag, on Sydney's North Shore. It is probable that she appropriated the family of her university friend, Colleen Olliffe, who lived in a modest suburb. Colleen's father, like Mr Miles, was in the printing business but did not have the rather austere personality of Madeleine's father.

The novel was clearly set in a fictionalised version of the David Jones department store in Elizabeth Street, Sydney. The interplay of the saleswomen (who dressed in black in 1960, when the novel is set, just as they do now) is so convincing, so comprehensively realised, that I assumed Madeleine had a holiday job there while a student, but she insisted this was not the case, 'although I often went shopping there with my mother'.

Madeleine's subsequent novels, *A Pure Clear Light*, *The Essence of the Thing* (nominated for the Booker) and *Stairway to Paradise*, are, I think, equally superb – though none have the warmth and pervasive good humour of *The Women in Black* – and mark her as a major writer. The palette is small, but the observation and the dialogue acute, touching and often very funny. A fastidious stylist, whose model was Jane Austen, she created, or re-created, a section of late twentieth-century London society in a manner similar to Austen's world of the nineteenth century. I remain astonished at the fidelity with which Madeleine captured the manners and mores of the middle-class English as I was never aware that she knew many of these people. I assume that her years working in bookshops introduced them to her and her interpretive genius took over from there.

If Madeleine's social circle was not wide, there were a number of devoted friends who seemed to be able to cope with her changes of mood, her demands and general waspishness. Perhaps her fervent Christianity, acquired sometime after she dispensed with Swami Ji, supplied her with a moral code that meant she often found others wanting. At some point most friends and relatives were cast off. A few managed a comeback but many, especially relatives, were in permanent outer darkness. Agents and publishers were almost saintly in the way they dealt with Madeleine's tantrums, her obsession with detail. She was aware, I realise, that a major strength of her writing was the accumulation of minutiae. She was so furious over some minor point in a French translation of one of her novels that she refused to allow it to appear. Kamikaze-like, she stipulated in her will that there were to be no translations of her novels into any language.

With a terrible sense of foreboding I sent her the screenplay of *The Women in Black*, written by Sue Milliken and myself. To my surprise, astonishment rather, she made no comment other than saying she looked forward to seeing the film. Perhaps she felt that if I could make a success of the intimate character studies of *Driving Miss Daisy* and *Tender Mercies* then I could do it again with her novel. It must have been a struggle, but she kept her reservations, and I can't believe they were not numerous, to herself.

Unlike so many of Madeleine's friends and associates I escaped being sent to Siberia – probably because I was only in London occasionally, was a link with university days (she enjoyed talking about our contemporaries) and shared Madeleine's interest in music. We even managed a visit to the Royal Albert Hall to hear Mitsuko Uchida play the Schumann Piano Concerto. Somehow, I engineered Madeleine down four flights of stairs in Notting Hill into a taxi, and then, complete with large oxygen cylinder, into a box near the stage. On another occasion, I arranged to take her to dinner at the Ivy so that she could meet an American film-maker she admired, Whit Stillman – the writer-director of three witty character-driven films dealing with middle-class Americans, *The Last Days of Disco*, *Metropolitan* and *Barcelona*. Whit, a handsome young man, was polite but clearly bewildered by this tiny person with dyed red hair, an oxygen cylinder, and forceful opinions. I also introduced her to my son, Adam, then a classics student at Balliol, and found myself somewhat bored as they discussed, at length, Adam's theory as to the identity of Shakespeare's Mr W.H. Madeleine assured Adam he had no idea what he was talking about.

Madeleine was always capable of surprising me. Her wild enthusiasm for the TV series *Buffy, the Vampire Slayer* seemed to me totally out of character. I found a few episodes on DVD and failed, still fail, to see why this nonsense would have interested her. But then I have all of Willie Nelson's discs and my friends can't equate that with my passion for opera.

On one of my visits to London, a year or so before Madeleine died, there was no answer at the flat, so I feared the worst. Through her former literary agent, Sarah Lutyens, I tracked her down in a hospital on the Kings Road. She was in a surprisingly stylish public ward with a TV set suspended over the bed and numerous tubes connecting her to all sorts of sci-fi machines. Never one to complain about her unenviable health she remained cheerful. She enjoyed meeting the other patients and nurses and hearing the stories of their lives. She told me her blood count.

'Is that good?' I asked.

'My doctor says that for me it's very good,' she replied. 'If it was anyone else they'd be dead.'

That was the last time I saw her. We spoke on the phone a few more times, then an email arrived, in June 2006, saying she had died. She must have been bitterly disappointed that I had directed numerous other scripts but not yet *The Women in Black*, but affected indifference. She also minimised the acclaim she had received for *The Essence of the Thing*, although it cannot fail to have meant a lot to her.

On her desk was a hundred pages or so of a new novel – a few typed but many in longhand and unnumbered. With the help of Sarah Lutyens the pages were arranged in their probable correct order. There are many characteristically witty and touching scenes, but the manuscript is too fragmentary for publication. Her will left her modest estate, as well as future royalties from her books, to charity. I was named her literary executor, in addition to which she left me a charming drawing, by Bernard Hesling, of the Sydney Conservatorium of Music. Various friends shared out her modest collection of books.

The angry cat was no problem as it had predeceased her.

'Is that good?' I asked.

'Her doctor says that treatment's very good,' she replied. 'But for anyone else they'd be dead.'

That was the last time I saw her. We spoke on the phone a few more times, then an email arrived, in June 2005, saying she had died. She must have been bitterly disappointed that [illegible] numerous [illegible] *The Women in Black*, [illegible] indifference; she also [illegible] the acclaim she had received for *The Essence of the Thing*, although it cannot fail to have given pleasure to her.

On her desk was a hundred pages or so of a new novel – a few thousand words in longhand and [illegible]. With the help of Sarah Lutyens the pages were arranged in their probable correct order. There are many characteristically witty and touching scenes, but the manuscript is too fragmentary for publication. Her will left her modest estate, as well as future royalties from her books, to charity. I was named her literary executor, in addition to which she left me a charming drawing by Richard [illegible] of the Sydney Conservatorium of Music. Various friends shared out her modest collection of books.

The angry cat was no problem as it had predeceased her.

The Women in Black

1

At the end of a hot November day Miss Baines and Mrs Williams of the Ladies' Frocks Department at Goode's were complaining to each other while they changed out of their black frocks before going home. 'Mr Ryder's not so bad,' said Miss Baines, in reference to the floor manager; 'it's that Miss Cartright who's a pain in the neck, excuse my French.' Miss Cartright was the buyer, and she never seemed to give them a moment's peace.

Mrs Williams shrugged and began to powder her nose. 'She always gets worse at this time of the year,' she pointed out. 'She wants to make sure we earn our Christmas bonus.' 'As if we could help it!' said Miss Baines. 'We're run off our feet!' Which was quite true: the great festival being now only six weeks away, the crowds of customers were beginning to surge and the frocks to vanish from the rails in an ever-faster flurry, and when Mrs Williams was washing out her undies in the handbasin that night she had a sudden sensation that her life was slipping away with the rinsing water as it gurgled down the plughole; but she pulled herself together and went on with her chores, while the Antipodean summer night throbbed outside all around her.

Mrs Williams, Patty, and Miss Baines, Fay, worked together with Miss Jacobs on Ladies' Cocktail Frocks, which was next to Ladies' Evening Frocks, down at the end of the second floor of Goode's Department Store in the centre of Sydney. F.G. Goode, a sharp Mancunian, had opened his original Emporium (Ladies' and Gents' Apparel – All the Latest London Modes) at the end of the last century, and had never looked back, because the people of the colony, he saw straightaway, would spend pretty well all they had in order to convince themselves that they were in the fashion. So now his grandchildren were the principal shareholders in a concern which turned over several million Australian £s every year, selling the latest London modes, and any modes from other sources which looked likely. Italian modes were in the ascendancy at present. 'I got it at Goode's', as the caption said, on that insufferable drawing of a superior-looking lady preening herself in a horribly smart new frock before the envious and despairing gaze of her friend – the frocks and the poses might change with the years, but that ad always ran in the bottom left-hand corner of the women's page in the *Herald*: I believe the space was booked in perpetuity: and the caption had long since become a city-wide catchphrase. Goode's stayed ahead of the competition by means of a terrific dedication to the modes. They sent the buying talent abroad for special training at the great department stores of London and New York. When the new season's clothes came into the shop twice a year the staff worked overtime, pricing and displaying, exclaiming the while. 'Never mind if it does retail at £9.17.6,' said Miss Cartright; 'this model will vanish within a fortnight – you mark my words!' And this they duly did.

2

Mrs Williams was a little, thin, straw-coloured woman with a worn-out face and a stiff-looking permanent wave. Her husband Frank was a bastard, naturally. He had married her when she was only twenty-one and he a strapping healthy twenty-six and why they had failed to produce any children was anyone's guess, but here it was ten years after the event and still she was working although the house was now fully furnished, furnished within an inch of its life in fact, and there was no particular need for the money, which she was saving up in the Bank of New South Wales, not knowing what else to do with it, while Frank continued to give her the housekeeping money which as a point of honour she spent entire, buying a lot of rump steak where other people in her situation might have bought mince and sausages, because Frank did like steak. She would get home from Goode's (they lived in a little house in Randwick) at about six o'clock, and take the steak out of the fridge. She did the vegetables and set the table. Just before seven Frank would get in, slightly the worse for drink: 'Hoo-ray!' he would call on his way to the bathroom. There he would wash vigorously, and by the time he stomped into the kitchen-dining room the steak was sizzling.

'What's for tea, Patty?' he would ask. 'Steak,' she said. 'Steak again,' said he. Whenever she tried to give him anything else, even lamb chops ('There's no meat on these things,' said Frank, waving a bone in front of him) he complained. Mrs Williams didn't care; she'd lost her appetite years ago. At the weekends she visited her mother or one of her sisters; Frank drove her there and fetched her, and while she was 'jaw, jaw, jawing' he played golf on the public course at Kingsford or drank in a pub. He was a bastard of the standard-issue variety, neither cruel nor violent, merely insensitive and inarticulate.

Patty had in fact consulted a physician about her childlessness and had been assured that her own equipment was in perfect order. 'Of course,' said the physician, 'we cannot investigate this question properly without seeing your husband. The fault may lie there; indeed it probably does. He may even be sterile.' 'Gee,' said Patty, overwhelmed. 'I don't think he'll come at that.' She couldn't even mention the subject to him. 'How often do you have intercourse?' asked the physician. 'Well,' said Patty, 'not that often. He gets tired.' The fact was that Frank's attentions were desultory. The physician regarded his patient with some despair. It was too bad. Here was a woman well into her childbearing years with no baby to nurse: it was entirely unnatural. She had lost all her bloom and was therefore not likely to attract another man who might accomplish the necessary so if her husband failed to come up to scratch her life would be wasted. It was too bad, it really was. 'Well,' said he, 'just keep trying. Conception is essentially a tricky business. Maximise the chances as much as possible; you've got plenty of time yet.' She was thirty when this conversation took place and as she left the surgery, the physician looking idly at her back view thought, she'd clean up quite well with a new hairdo, some paint on her face and a black nightie; but the husband probably wouldn't notice, the bastard; and in this assumption he was probably correct. Frank worked in the sales department of the great roof-tile company whose vari-coloured wares were at this time so enticingly displayed in Parramatta Road; drank with his mates every night after work in a pub near Railway Square and then went home to Patty and his half pound of rump steak. After that, and watching Patty wash up, and a few frames of television, which had only recently arrived in the Commonwealth of Australia, he lumbered off to bed – 'Think I'll turn in' – where Patty – 'Okay dear' – followed him. She lay beside him in a blue nylon nightdress and soon she heard his snores.

The vacant child's room, painted primrose yellow so as to cover either eventuality, waited in vain for its tiny occupant, and Patty, in a state of unacknowledged and unwitting despair, went on working at Goode's, this year as all the previous years, until she had a baby on the way. 'I don't understand it, I really don't,' said her mother, Mrs Crown, not to Patty but to Patty's sister Joy. 'I don't think Frank's up to much,' said Joy darkly. 'Oh, go on,' said her mother. 'He's a fine strapping fellow.' 'Looks aren't everything,' said Joy. 'I don't understand it, I really don't,' said Mrs Crown. 'Never you mind,' said Joy. Joy was younger than Patty and already had two; Patty was the one in the middle; their elder sister Dawn had three. There was obviously nothing wrong with the Crown breeding ability. Joy thought Patty never should have married Frank. In the meantime, when she wanted something special, a party frock for example, Patty got her the staff discount at Goode's by pretending that the frock was for herself, which it obviously wasn't if you were looking, because it was an SW and Patty took an SSW, but no one ever noticed.

3.

Patty and Fay, and Miss Jacobs (whose Christian name remained a secret) all arrived at Goode's Staff Entrance by twenty to nine in the morning, as they were meant to do, except that Fay once in a while was late, and looked it – harried and untidy. They went up to the top of the building (Staff and Administration) in the Staff Lift and went to the Staff Locker Room (past Accounts) to change into their black frocks, which were hanging in their lockers where they had left them on the previous night after changing to go home.

These black frocks were worn through the week and dry-cleaned by Goode's over the weekend ready to start another week's work on Monday morning, and smelt peculiar. Not nasty, but different – simply the result of the smell of frequent dry-cleaning, mingled with the scent of cheap talcum powder and sweat. Every Goode's assistant had this smell while she was wearing her black frock.

These garments, which were supplied by Goode's who retained

ownership, were designed to flatter both the fuller and the thinner figure and truly enhanced neither, but then, Goode's assistants were not there to decorate the shop but to sell its wares. So each woman climbed into her black frock with a sigh of resignation, twitching hopelessly at it to make it sit better while regarding her reflection in the full-length mirror. The frocks were made of rayon crepe in a somewhat late 1930s style, which had been retained because it was neat in outline and used relatively little cloth.

Patty Williams's frock was an SSW as we know, whereas Fay Baines was an SW, but Miss Jacobs was a perfect OSW, especially around the bust. Her size and her general appearance were pretty well the only things about Miss Jacobs which could be known; everything else was a mystery. 'That Miss Jacobs,' said Fay to her friend Myra in Repin's where they were drinking iced coffee, 'is a real mystery.' Even Miss Cartright found a moment now and then to wonder about Miss Jacobs, who had never missed a single day's work through either illness or misadventure. Who was she: where did she live and eat and sleep: what was her existence outside the opening hours of F.G. Goode's? No one there had the merest idea, except for the Wages Department who knew where she lived but declined to share the information should anyone think of asking, which they didn't. Miss Jacobs left Goode's every evening in the skirt and blouse (and if it was winter, the jacket or coat) in which she had arrived, carrying a large string bag with a brown paper-wrapped parcel or two within it. What was in these parcels, for example? No one could say. She walked away down Castlereagh Street in the direction of the Quay: which could mean all kinds of places from Hunter's Hill (unlikely) to Manly (just possible).

Miss Jacobs, stout and elderly, had a swarthy face and exiguous dark grey hair tied into a small antique-looking bun at the back of her large round head. She wore glasses with steel frames and always had a clean white handkerchief tucked into her bosom. She wore black lace-up shoes with cuban heels and had a stompy rather pathetic walk. Mr Ryder caught up with her in Pitt Street one evening and attempted to accompany her for some distance in a spirit of friendliness, but whether for necessity or not, she parted from him at the very next corner and walked away alone down Martin Place, muttering a word about Wynyard, but Mr Ryder thought this must be a put-up job because he himself travelled via Wynyard and had never seen Miss Jacobs in the vicinity thereof.

Miss Jacobs had not only worked at Goode's for longer than Mrs Williams (who had started after leaving school in Children's and transferred to Ladies' four years ago) but was also rather important to the scheme of things in Ladies' Cocktail, because she was in charge of alterations, which you could probably tell by the fact that she always wore a long tape-measure around her neck, so as to be ready for the ladies who wanted hems adjusted or even seams: the assistant who was serving such a lady would come out of the fitting room saying 'Miss Jacobs, Miss Jacobs please? Alteration here when you're free!' and Miss Jacobs would look up from the hem she was pinning in another fitting room and say around the pins in her mouth, 'All in good time, I've only got one pair of hands. And legs, for the matter of that.' And the lady she was pinning would smile, or titter, in sympathy, as it were. When the frock was pinned it would go up to the seventh floor for sewing by one of the alteration hands and when it was done (it might have to wait its turn for a few days) it would be delivered, like so much of Goode's merchandise ('Send it, please') in one of Goode's blue and yellow vans, which were a familiar sight in all the better-class suburbs of Sydney:

F.G. Goode's
Serving the People of Sydney since 1895.

Miss Jacobs had been serving the people, at any rate the ladies, of Sydney since *before the war* – that utterly legendary and even fabulous era. She had started in Gloves and Hosiery, done a stint in Ladies' Day Frocks (where she was taught to take charge of alterations) and then gone down to Ladies' Sportswear and Casuals, but she had not cared for the tone of this department very much, and had been glad to come back to the second floor when a vacancy occurred in Ladies' Cocktail, where she had now been ever since the New Look, tape-measure at the ready, and a box of pins to hand.

4

Fay Baines was twenty-nine if she was a day, and Patty Williams wondered if she might not actually be thirty, and that wasn't all that she wondered. For whereas Patty had Frank to talk about, albeit there was virtually nothing to say ('Frank played golf on Sunday') and beyond that her house ('I think I'll have loose covers made for the suite. I want a new vacuum cleaner') to say nothing of her mother ('It's Mum's birthday on Friday; we're all going over Saturday') or her sisters ('Dawn . . . Joy'), Fay Baines talked about nothing but *men*.

It was chronic; this one and that one: going out here, and there, and all over the place, with Tom, Dick and Harry: and was there any sign at all that any of them might be thinking of marrying her? Not on your life. Patty sometimes wondered if Tom, Dick and Harry, not to mention Bill, Bruce and Bob were all quite real. After all, the woman was thirty if she was a day.

In any case it wasn't quite nice, when you came to think about it, because Fay lived by herself, all alone in a flatette near Bondi

Junction, apparently; so there was no one, like a mother, to keep an eye on things and make certain that Fay didn't go too far, which Patty suspected she just might do, being at least thirty-one, or at any rate no spring chicken, and obviously desperate, not that anyone wouldn't be in her situation, but anyway men took advantage, being interested in only one thing; unless they were Frank.

She aired all these cogitations to Joy, Dawn and their mother, omitting the rider about Frank, and they all agreed, eating sponge-cake at the kitchen table while the children ran about Mrs Crown's small back garden, if one might so dignify a rectangle of couch grass and a spindly gum tree with an empty old rabbit hutch next to it.

'She should share a proper flat with some other girls,' said Mrs Crown, 'like Dawn used to, before she got married.' 'Yeah, no thanks to *you*, Mum,' said Dawn, somewhat heatedly. There had been the most awful row about that move out into the world: Mrs Crown had accused Dawn of all sorts of evil desires and intentions when Dawn had announced that she was leaving home to share a flat with two friends, when all Dawn had wanted was some privacy. How her mother had carried on! Now she was talking as if it was the most natural thing in the world. Typical! 'Well,' said Mrs Crown, cutting herself some more cake, 'times change, don't they?' 'No,' said Joy in her irritating way, 'people do.' 'Anyway,' said Patty, 'Fay Baines should share a flat and not live alone, if she cares about her reputation. That's my opinion. What would a man think, a girl living all alone like that?' And the four women sat and reflected for a moment, envisioning exactly what a man would think.

Fay Baines, *pace* Patty Williams, was in fact twenty-eight years old, an SW with a tendency to become a W if she didn't watch herself, and while Mrs Crown and her three daughters were indulging in their impertinent speculations, eating cake the while, she was sitting in an armchair crying into a small white handkerchief. It was one of a set of four which she had been given, all folded in a flat gold cardboard box, by one of her admirers.

When she wasn't crying she was a handsome girl, with wavy dark hair and large innocent brown eyes, and she was fond of cosmetics, which she applied quite copiously, especially when going out. 'You look good enough to eat,' Fred Fisher had said, the first time he came to pick her up. When they got home again he did begin to eat her, or as near as makes no difference, and she had had her work cut out fending him off. Then he called her an ugly name and left in a temper. This was the sort of thing which happened to Fay, who never seemed to meet the sort of man she dreamed of: someone who would respect her as well as desiring her: someone who would love her and wish to marry her. Somehow the sight of Fay was not one which inspired thoughts of marriage, and this was grievous, for Fay wished for nothing else: which was natural, everything considered. Meanwhile men were forever getting the wrong idea, just as Mrs Crown and her daughters suggested they would.

Fay was pretty well alone in the world: her mother, a war widow, had died some years ago and her brother – who was married with two children – lived in Melbourne, where once in a while she visited him. But she did not get on with his wife, who in Fay's opinion gave herself airs, and these visits became less and less frequent. 'If at first you don't succeed,' said Fay to herself, 'try, try, try again.' Someone had written this on the first page of her autograph book when she was in her teens and it had made a lasting impression.

Fay, wanting to be a showgirl, had soon had to settle for being variously a cigarette girl and a cocktail waitress during her late teens and early twenties; and when she was twenty-three she had met Mr Marlow, a rich and middle-aged bachelor. Two years later he had given her £500 in cash and told her that he was going to live in Perth and that it had been wonderful knowing her. She had stayed in the solitary flatette, now no longer essential, out of sheer inertia; forsaking the rackety life of the cocktail waitress with its peculiar hours and large tips she had gone to work in a dress shop in the Strand Arcade. There she had made the acquaintance of Mr Green, a frock manufacturer; when he suddenly announced that he was getting married she as suddenly forsook the Strand Arcade with all its memories and went to work at Goode's, where she had now been for just over eighteen months.

The men she saw these days were a rag tag and bobtail collection of faces from her livelier past, blind dates organised by her friend Myra Parker (comrade and mentor since Fay's night-club days), and men whom she met at the parties to which she was taken by Myra, or by the rag tag and bobtail. And the £500? That was in the bank. She intended to splash it all on her trousseau, when the time came. Sometimes, as now, she found herself crying, because the time was so long in coming that she could fearfully suspect that it might never do so, but after a while, when her hanky was all used up and sopping, she dried her eyes, washed her face and lit a Craven A. 'If at first you don't succeed,' she told herself, 'try, try, try again.' She was a brave girl, like most of her compatriots.

5

The great glass and mahogany entrance doors of F.G. Goode's were opened promptly at five past nine every morning, Monday to Saturday, and for the rest of the day until 5.30 (or on Saturdays, 12.30) the ladies went in and out with their desires and their fulfilments. Most of the ladies arrived on foot; if they were very smartly dressed the doorman in his uniform of a lieutenant-colonel in the Ruritanian Army would touch his cap or perhaps give a slight nod; if they arrived by taxi or, goodness me, chauffeur-driven car, he would spring to the kerbstone and open the door and hold it while the lady emerged.

Most ladies, whatever their primary business, lingered on the ground floor before ascending by lift or escalator, casing the perfume counter, the gloves, the handkerchiefs, the scarves and the belts and handbags. Sometimes they went straight to the soda fountain and sat at the marble-topped counter on a gold stool drinking a milkshake or an ice-cream soda because Sydney is a very big city and such ladies might have travelled far to get to

Goode's. They might take a headache powder with their soda to set themselves up for the day ahead.

If it was the school holidays they might have a kiddy or two with them and those were the ladies for whom even a Ruritanian army officer might feel sorry – ghastly brats, these kids, who fought with each other and began every sentence with the words 'I want . . . ' Most of these kiddies were here for the shoes, because the Children's Shoes Department had an X-ray machine so that you could be sure their foot bones were not pushed out of alignment by their new shoes, and this machine was extremely popular with the better-class mother, until it was discovered that the effect of all those X-rays was somewhat more dangerous than wearing improperly-fitting shoes, dire as that most surely was.

If the kiddies behaved themselves moderately well they were taken when all the shopping was done to have lunch in the restaurant on the fifth floor, which was therefore not a nice place to be during the school holidays, for the kiddies tended to play up just as soon as they were safely seated, very few mothers having the face to march them out again once they were, so that these luncheons were punctuated by squeals and slaps and spilt drinks and shattered jellies; and fewer mothers yet had the *savoir-faire* to leave a tip commensurate with the mayhem caused.

Miss Jacobs, Mrs Williams and Miss Baines were all spared the worst of these aspects of life within the walls of Goode's because very few ladies thought of trying to buy a cocktail frock or even a day frock with their little ones in tow. Up here, all was *luxe calme et volupté*, with nice pink lights and pink-tinted mirrors which made you look just lovely, and the thick grey silence underfoot of finest Axminster.

The women in black were all at their stations ready to face the summer day by nine o'clock precisely, when Miss Cartright came swishing over to them in her coin-spotted cotton pique. 'Girls!' she cried. How they detested that. It was rumoured that she had been Head Prefect at PLC and couldn't they just imagine it. Such side! Here she was. Now what?

'One of the temporary staff will be joining you next week,' said Miss Cartright with a bright smile. 'I hope you'll make her welcome. I know you don't usually have a temp in this section, but I think she will be useful, and she can help Magda out as well.'

Oh, *gawd.*

At the very end of the Ladies' Frocks Department, past Cocktail Frocks, there was something very special, something quite, quite wonderful; but it wasn't for everybody: that was the point. Because there, at the very end, there was a lovely arch, on which was written in curly letters '*Model Gowns*'. And beyond the arch was a rose-pink cave illuminated by frilly little lamps and furnished with a few elegant little sofas upholstered in oyster-grey brocade; and the walls were lined with splendid mahogany cupboards in which hung, on pink satin-covered hangers, the actual Model Gowns, whose fantastic prices were all in guineas.

To one side of the cave there was a small Louis XVI-style table and chair, where ladies could write cheques or sign sales dockets, and to each side was a great cheval glass where a lady having donned a Model Gown (did she dare) in one of the large and commodious fitting rooms might look at herself properly, walking around and turning, to get the effect of the frock in the sort of proper big space where it would ultimately be seen. A chandelier hung from the ceiling; almost the only fitment lacking to the scene was the bottle of Veuve Clicquot foaming at the mouth and the tulip-shaped glass; in all other respects the cave was a faithful reproduction of the luxurious space in which its clients were to be supposed continually to have their being: and the pythoness who guarded the cave was Magda.

Magda, the luscious, the svelte and full-bosomed, the beautifully-tailored and manicured and coiffed, was the most overwhelming, scented, gleaming, *god-awful* and ghastly snake-woman that Mrs Williams, Miss Baines and even, probably, Miss Jacobs herself had ever seen, or even imagined. *Magda* (no one could even try to pronounce her frightful Continental surname) was just a terrible fact of life which you ignored most of the time, but if they were going to share a temp with Magda they knew who would be doing most of the sharing: they were going to have Magda slithering out of her pink cave and sliding over to Ladies' Cocktail and pinching that temp away from them just the minute she showed herself useful: that was a *fact*, because Magda was the kind of woman who always got what she wanted: you could tell. Because Magda (gawd help us) was *a Continental*: and weren't they glad *they* weren't.

At least Mrs Williams was; she was quite definite about that. Gawd, she said; I couldn't stand to get about like that. Miss Jacobs simply looked more than usually affronted, even slightly offended, as if she had just seen a spider in her teacup. Fay Baines thought her frightful, just frightful, the way she walked, and that: but at home in front of her mirror she wondered seriously just what sort of make-up Magda used and how she put it on, because the woman was forty if she was a day, and she looked – you had to hand it to her – she looked terrific. You had to hand it to her.

6

When Lesley Miles arrived for her interview for a position as Sales Assistant (Temporary) at Goode's, she was given a form to fill in, and the first word she wrote on it, very carefully and with a spooky sense of danger, was 'Lisa'.

This was the name she had chosen for herself several years before: she disliked the one she had been given more than she could say, and had long since resolved to take another at the first opportunity. This was the first opportunity.

'Lisa Miles!' cried a voice; and Lesley-Lisa sprang to her feet and followed a woman into the small room where the interviews were being conducted. 'Well, Lisa,' said the woman – and Lesley's new life, as Lisa, commenced. How very simple it was: she was sure she would get used to it immediately. She sat up very straight, like a Lisa, and smiled gaily. Now it would all begin.

Miss Cartright, who was conducting the interview, looked piercingly at the teenager seated before her: one had to be careful to get the right kind of girl here at Goode's, even if she was only a temporary hired for the Christmas rush and the New Year Sales which followed. This one was at least evidently intelligent: the form she had completed showed that she was about to sit for the Leaving Certificate. But what a face! what a figure! She had the body and the mien of a child of around fifteen, and an immature one at that: small and thin, even skinny, with frizzy blonde hair and bright innocent eyes behind utilitarian-looking spectacles. Still, she would look more adult in the black frock: her own clothes were impossible – obviously home-made, and not well-made either: a little cotton print frock, with badly set-in sleeves, and a peter-pan collar. Poor kid.

Lisa, having ironed her pink frock – which was her best – with the greatest care, and wearing her high-heeled shoes with a brand new pair of nylon stockings, was confident that her appearance approached the condition of Lisa-ness as nearly as was possible in all the circumstances, and sat on, smiling and eager and absolutely oblivious of Miss Cartright's inner thoughts.

'And what are you thinking of doing, Lisa,' asked Miss Cartright, 'when you leave school?' 'Well, I'm going to wait and see what my Leaving results are,' said Lisa, looking vague. 'I don't suppose you mean to make a career in the retail trade?' said Miss Cartright. 'Oh, no!' cried Lisa. Miss Cartright laughed. 'It's quite all right, Lisa. It doesn't suit everybody. But as long as you are working here, you will be expected to work hard, and *as if* it were your permanent job. Do you understand that?' 'Oh, *of course*,' said Lisa, desperately. '*Of course*; I do understand. I'll work very hard.' And Miss Cartright, thinking it might be rather quaint to see the girl in such a context, decided to put her in Ladies' Cocktail, where she could give a hand to Magda in Model Gowns now and then, because although she looked so childish, she was evidently bright as well as willing, and might be quite useful, all things considered. 'You start on the first Monday in December, then,' she informed the new Sales Assistant (Temporary), 'and your wages will be paid fortnightly, on Thursdays. Now we will go and see about your black frock.' It was only now that she realised that it was very unlikely that there would be a frock which would fit this skinny child. Oh, well: perhaps she would grow into it, once the strain of the examinations was behind her. Lisa followed her from the room, up the fire stairs to the Wardrobe Room, and so enchanted was she at the idea of wearing black that she did not care in the very least that the frock she was given was one size too large, she being an XXSSW; for in any case, she had never ever had a frock which fitted properly.

The interviews for temporary staff had been held on a Saturday afternoon, after Goode's – and every other shop in the city – had closed for the weekend, and Lisa had arrived just at closing time, when the streets were still busy with people going home or to the pictures or to restaurants. Now, a good hour later, she emerged from the Staff Entrance into the city in its Saturday afternoon and Sunday condition: so silent, so deserted as to suggest a terrible and universal disaster: the visitation of some dreadful plague, or of the Angel, even, of Death itself. Each footfall could be heard as she walked down Pitt Street and Martin Place; as she passed the GPO she saw a woman posting a letter, and in George Street she saw a man in the far distance, going towards Circular Quay; the streets were otherwise quite empty. She walked down the dark mysterious concourse of Wynyard Station towards the trains, and by the time her own arrived, there were only three other passengers on the platform. She had never before been in town on a Saturday afternoon, and the episode, following upon the novelty of the interview for her very first job, induced a feeling of awful strangeness – and yet, of a certain ghostly familiarity: for Lisa believed herself to be in all likelihood a poet, and this experience seemed to her to be one about which one could certainly find oneself writing a poem, as long as one could manage to recall this feeling, this apprehension, of a world transformed, and oneself in it and with it: a sensation and an apprehension for which, for the moment, she had no precise words. Lisa, she said to herself, sitting in the train as it rattled across the Bridge. My name is Lisa Miles. The feeling of strangeness was still within her, and equally, she within it, as she knocked on the door of the house in Chatswood where she lived with her parents – she had as yet no key. Her mother opened the door. 'Hello Lesley!' she said.

In the few weeks between the ending of the Leaving Certificate examinations and her first day at Goode's, Lisa went to the Blue Mountains with her mother, read *Tender is the Night* and part of *Anna Karenina*, went twice to the pictures, and most of all stood silent and impatient while her mother, making her some new clothes, adjusted pins. 'Stand still,' she commanded. 'You want to look nice, don't you? It's your first job.'

'Yes, but I'll be wearing *a black frock*,' said Lisa. 'They won't see me in my own clothes.' 'They will when you arrive and when you go home,' said her mother. 'It won't matter then,' said Lisa. 'It always matters,' said Mrs Miles. 'Tyger! Tyger! burning bright / In the forests of the night,' Lisa began. 'Oh, you and your tiger,' said her mother. 'Don't distract me: and *stay still*.'

Lisa was an only child, and this fact was believed by onlookers to account for her general queerness. Her father was a compositor on the *Herald* and was rarely to be seen, generally arriving home in the wee small hours, sleeping till the afternoon and going off to a pub to drink beer for an hour or two until it was time to go to work. During his waking hours on Saturday he glued himself to the wireless to listen to the racing, having placed several off-course bets: Mrs Miles had not the slightest idea of the size of his salary, and would have been stunned if anyone had told her.

If she had known how great a proportion of it ended up in the pockets of the off-course bookmakers she would have fainted dead away.

She had not known him well when they married, during the war: he was a handsome soldier at a dance she had attended, and when he had suggested after a brief acquaintance that they make a go of it, she had seen no reason at all to say no. She had until then had a hard life, for she had been born into a bakery business, and had been covered with flour since the age of eleven when she had been drafted in to assist her elders as soon as she came home from school. She was shown how to put the glace cherries on the fairy cakes, and subsequently instructed in more difficult operations, until by the age of fifteen there was almost nothing she didn't know about fancy baking. At this stage she left school and joined her family at their trade on a full-time basis. She was paid a derisory wage, in cash, and continued to live at home, over the shop: she might still have been covered with flour to this day if her Ted hadn't come along in his smart military outfit. Once that was removed, he had less to say for himself; but that was life, wasn't it. She might have felt as badly as she suspected his doing, that she had not provided him with a son, were it not that her Lesley was the utter apple of her eye.

7

Magda and Stefan had sat up very late playing cards with two friends on the Sunday night before the first Monday in December, and by the time Magda had cleared away the dirty glasses and emptied the ashtrays and generally straightened the living room, and then made her *démaquillage*, it was past two a.m. She stood and looked out at Mosman Bay for a minute and sighed, and retired to bed. Stefan was reading a page of Nietzsche, as was his wont last thing at night. 'Ah Magda, my beloved,' said he, flinging aside his book, 'a woman's work is never done until I am almost asleep myself. Come into bed now.' 'There is no law in this country,' said Magda, 'against men helping their wives to clear up the mess, is there?' 'As a matter of fact,' said Stefan, 'I think there is.' 'You are probably right,' Magda agreed, as she got into bed; and it was easily three a.m. when at last her eyes closed in sleep.

The consequence was that when she looked into her mirror having risen at her usual hour the next morning, she looked a perfect fright, and she spent the next fifteen minutes lying on the sofa with her feet higher than her head, and with two large slices of cucumber covering her closed eyelids. Then she got up with a great sigh and ate some yoghurt, and got ready for work.

It will not be imagined that Magda wore the regulation Goode's black frock while presiding over the Model Gowns: no: in this matter (as in several others) a compromise had been achieved whereby Magda agreed to wear black, but on her own terms. She had acquired a collection of suitable black frocks and what she called costumes, many of which were relieved, not to say enhanced, by discreet additions of white – collars, it might be, or cuffs, or both – or even, in the case of one costume, pale pink; all of which had been craftily purchased by Magda from the sort of expensive little shops which she preferred to patronise at a large trade discount further subsidised as per their agreement by Goode's. 'When I was *vendeuse* at Patou,' Magda had remarked, 'I wore nothing but Patou. Naturally.' This was an absolute whopper, because in the first place, Magda had never been a *vendeuse* at Patou. However, she might have been; it was a good and serviceable story which had as much as anything else she had to say secured her the job of taking charge of the Model Gowns. 'These people,' Magda would often say to her Continental friends, 'know *nothing*.'

Magda went up to the Staff Locker Room not, therefore, to change, but to put away her handbag and to tidy herself, walking past her inglorious colleagues in a cloud of Mitsoukou. She patted powder onto her nose, apparently oblivious of the sneers of onlookers, and turning around, gave them a dazzling smile. 'A beautiful day, is it not?' she asked. 'I have enjoyed the journey here this morning so greatly. How lucky we all are, to live in such a place.' And she left the room, walking past a frieze of faces which were dumbstruck with astonishment, incomprehension, and contempt: reactions which strained for articulation as her steps retreated through the door. 'Stone the crows,' said Patty Williams, voicing the thoughts of all of them.

It was at this moment that Lisa made her appearance. She stood, hesitant, in the doorway, frail as a fairy, in a gathered skirt and what might have been a white school blouse. Patty Williams glanced at her and turned to Fay Baines. 'Now look what the cat's dragged in,' she observed. 'Are you looking for someone,' she called out, 'or are you lost? This is staff only.' 'I am,' said Lisa. 'I mean, I'm staff. I'm a temporary.' 'Gawd strewth,' said Patty *sotto voce* to Fay. 'Have you got a locker number?' she asked Lisa. Lisa told her the number she had just been given at Staff Reception and Patty stared. 'Oh, that's just along here. Gawd,' she said again to Fay. 'That must be our new temp. Now I've seen everything. Come along and get changed then,' she said, raising her voice again; 'it's time to go downstairs. There's no dawdling here, you know,' she added, sternly. It was wonderful how assertive Patty could be when she had no fear of serious opposition, and for the next week she made Lisa's hours of work just as frantic as she knew how.

It was Miss Jacobs who had the seniority and therefore strictly speaking the right to harry Lisa, or at least to make sure that she learned the routines and made herself useful, but what with Christmas and New Year and all the parties coming up, and consequently all the cocktail frocks vanishing off the rails and into the fitting rooms quicker than you could say *knife*, Miss Jacobs had her work cut out with pinning up the alterations; Patty had virtually a clear field for the exercise of her power and she grew into the role most famously.

'Just left school have you, Lisa?' she asked. 'Just done the Inter, eh? Did you pass?' 'I've just done the Leaving,' said Lisa. 'Well!' said Patty, disconcerted and even appalled. '*The Leaving*. Well. I thought you were fifteen, or about that. The Leaving!' Patty looked incredulously and even fearfully at the *wunderkind*. 'You want to be a teacher, do you?' said she. 'Oh no, I don't think so,' said Lisa. 'I'm going,' she said, believing that she was obliged to offer a truthful account of herself, 'to be a poet. I think,' and she trailed off, vaguely, noticing now the horrible effect of her candour. 'A poet!' exclaimed Patty. 'Jeez: a poet!' She turned to Fay, who was spiking a document at the conclusion of a sale. 'Did you hear that?' she asked. 'Lisa here is going to be *a poet*!' And she smiled evilly. 'No, I mean,' amended the confused girl, 'I'd like to *try* to be a poet. Or perhaps,' she added, in the hope of deflecting Patty's amazement, 'an actress.'

'An actress!' cried Patty. '*An actress*!' And Lisa saw at once that she had only magnified her initial error, and that she was now suddenly an object of open ridicule; for the appearance she presented in her black frock and utilitarian spectacles, thin and childish, was so far from their conception of the actress that the two women both now burst into laughter. Lisa stood helpless before them, and began to blush; she was even on the verge of tears.

Fay was the first to compose herself; she at any rate had recollections of her own attempt at a stage career to still her derision. 'It's real hard to get into the theatre,' she said kindly. 'You have to know someone. Do you know anyone?' 'No,' said Lisa in a small voice. And then she had a sudden and brilliant inspiration. 'Not *yet*,' she added.

Miss Jacobs had overheard this conversation without appearing to do so, standing a few yards away from the group writing out an Alterations Ticket. She turned around. 'That's right,' she said. 'She's still young. She doesn't know anyone *yet*. She's just a slip of a girl.' Miss Jacobs turned her back on the astonished silence which her utterance had created, and walked slowly to a nearby rail of cocktail frocks, which were meant to be arranged by size. 'I think some of these frocks are out of order,' she said, turning back to Lisa. 'Would you look through them, Lisa, and put them right? That's a good girl.'

Lisa, reading the sizes on the labels of the array of cocktail frocks, XSSW, SSW, SW, W, OW (there were only two OW's in this range), and placing them in the correct order where necessary, resorted to her usual vade-mecum in times of trial. 'Tyger! Tyger! burning bright,' she chanted silently to herself, 'In the forests of the night,' and she had just arrived at 'what dread feet?' when a customer whom she had not so much as noticed interrupted her. She held up a black-and-magenta sheath. 'Have you got this one,' she asked, 'in a W? I can only see this SSW here.' 'Just a minute,' said Lisa, 'and I'll enquire from the stockroom. I'm sorry,' she added, as she had been schooled by Patty to do, 'to keep you waiting.' Did he who made the Lamb make thee?

The tyger had entered Lisa's life, back in the days when she was no one but Lesley, three years previously, when she was at the beginning of her Intermediate Certificate year. Frail, apparently lonely, strangely disengaged, not much noticed by her teachers, a merely average performer academically, she had sat near the back of the classroom and faded into corners and against walls during recess. Her only cronies seemed to be two other girls similarly outside the fashion: a very fat girl and another who suffered from eczema: girls for whom there seemed everything to be done, but nothing which might be: girls who must find their way through the maze as best they might.

How the fat girl, the girl with eczema, accomplished this feat is not recorded; in the case of Lisa, the thread was discovered within the pages of a poetry anthology which came into her hands one day in the school library – literally: it fell off the shelf while she was searching for a quite different book, and since it opened as it fell, her eye could not help alighting on the right-hand page: where she espied the word, 'tyger'. This having come to pass, the rest followed with simple inevitability, for no moderately alert fourteen-year-old is going to see the word 'tyger', spelt thus so mysteriously, so enticingly, without investigating further, and as Lisa did so, the chasm of the poetic opened at her feet. She had soon got the poem by heart, and during the next few weeks she pondered its meaning, and even its means, and when a few months later her class was asked to choose a poem, any poem in the English language, and write an essay thereon, Lisa was in a position to say much on the subject of Blake's tyny masterpiece, and did so freely.

Her English teacher wondered aloud thereafter if she ought not to be sitting nearer the front of the classroom: it was possible, she thought, that the girl's eyesight made so great a distance from the blackboard inadvisable. Lisa was made to move to a desk in the second row, and went on as she had begun; for Miss Phipps had, as it were, now tasted blood. 'First-class honours material, definitely,' she said in the Staff Room. 'Didn't know she had it in her. First class, definitely.' It being the primary purpose of every teacher in the school to produce as many first-class honours results in the Leaving Certificate examinations as humanly possible, Lisa, all unknowingly, was now a marked child. As is the way of things, the attention and encouragement (discreet enough) which she now for the first time received affected her performance generally, and she improved in all her subjects. By the time she was in her last year, she was respectably in the ranks of the medium-to-high flyers: those students who would achieve not spectacular, but certainly solid, results, and almost certainly win Commonwealth Scholarships.

Filling in the application form for the last had been a matter not unproblematical. 'Well, I don't know, Lesley,' said her mother. 'I don't know about *the university*. We'll have to see what your dad says. He has to sign it anyway.' They managed to corner him just as he began to go off one evening to the *Sydney Morning Herald*. 'No daughter of mine is going anywhere near that cesspit,' said he; 'and that's final.' By the end of the following week, he had agreed to give his signature to the form on the understanding that if his daughter were by some extreme chance actually to gain the scholarship, there would nonetheless be no question whatever of her taking it up. 'It's for the school, really,' said Mrs Miles. 'They want her to do it at the school. It's good for their record.' 'Yes, well,' said E. Miles, compositor. 'I didn't want her going to that school anyway. A lot of stuck-up snobs.' Here he was animadverting to the fact that the academy in question, a State High School, admitted only children of a certain intelligence: Mrs Miles's delight when her Lesley had at the age of eleven found herself among their number had been one of many joys of parenthood which she had been unable, alas, to share with her co-author. She had had five years, now, of silent lamplit evenings, Lesley sitting doing her increasingly time-consuming homework at the kitchen table, her mother sitting on the cane chair, knitting or sewing or looking at *The Women's Weekly*, invisibly glowing with pride. Her girl: a scholar.

8

By the end of her first week as a Sales Assistant (Temporary) at Goode's, Lisa's appearance was more remarkably fragile than ever, and her black frock seemed to be nearer two sizes too large than one. Goodness me, thought Miss Cartright as she passed by Ladies' Cocktail, that child looks positively starved: it's hardly decent. 'Have you had your lunch hour yet?' she asked her later in the day. 'Oh, yes, thank you,' replied the child. 'Mind you eat a proper lunch then,' said Miss Cartright sternly. 'You need plenty of food to keep going here. That's why we subsidise the Staff Canteen you know, to see that you're all well fed. So mind you eat a proper lunch every day, Lisa.' 'Oh yes, of course,' replied she.

'Lesley,' said her mother, 'I don't want you eating that canteen food more than you can help. I'm sure it isn't good for you: you don't know where it's been, or who's been handling it. And it can't be fresh. I'll make you some nice sandwiches to take.' Her daughter didn't argue, for in fact although she had been pleased by the canteen's multi-coloured salads and trembling jellies with their tiny rosettes of whipped cream, she found the canteen itself and its clientele melancholy, and that not poetically so. By the end of her first week she had established a routine whereby, rushing up the fire stairs to the Staff Locker Room and changing back into her own clothes and fetching her sandwiches and a book, she was able having rushed down the same stairs to the street below and up Market Street and then across Elizabeth Street – barring cars, taxis and trams – to Hyde Park, to enjoy forty-five minutes in the embrace of its amorous green.

The weather was now abominably, relentlessly, hot, and she discovered that by sitting to one side or another, depending on the prevailing breeze, on the rim of the Archibald Fountain, she could enjoy its cooling spray as it was blown against her. Sitting thus, her stomach full of the hearty meat or cheese-filled sandwiches cut by her loving mother, her mind full of the anguish of the tale of A. Karenina which she was now very near finishing, she ascended into a state of wondering blissfulness which was induced to a large degree by the sheer novelty of being and acting quite alone: the exquisite experience of happy solitude.

It was while she was sitting thus on the Friday of that first week, her blouse now damp from the spray of the fountain and with but a few minutes remaining to her before she must rush back the way she had come and rehabilitate herself in her black frock, that Magda passed by and, having previously eyed Lisa from the portentous entrance to Model Gowns, hailed her.

'Ah, Lisa, I think, is it not? My name is Magda – you will have seen me without doubt presiding over our Model Gowns at Goode's, where we must now –' and here Magda consulted a diamond watch – 'return, I believe.' 'Oh yes, thank you,' Lisa stuttered in confusion. Magda's eye swept over her as she rose, gathering her book and her litter. What a tiny and half-made creature this was, who had been proposed to her as an assistant in her Model Gowns – should she need her. As if she might! – but come to think of it, she could be useful for one or two tedious little tasks: and in any case: if she were to spirit Lisa away from Ladies' Cocktail for a while it would spite those catty women who had the present charge of her. Well, she would do it, and soon, too. 'Dear Miss Cartright – she is so elegant, don't you agree? She has true style, unlike many women I see around me', and here Magda cast a great lustrous-eyed glance around her which comprehended everyone within a radius of one hundred yards, and sighed, but with resignation. 'She tells me I am to have the use of your no doubt excellent services during the next few weeks while I cope with my Christmas rush. Is that not so?' 'Well, yes,' said Lisa, 'I think she did tell me that I was to help you too sometimes.' 'Yes, well, we shall plan that in the next week,' said Magda, comfortably. 'In the meantime, I wonder why your back is wet. Have you been sweating?' 'Oh no!' cried Lisa, 'I've been sitting by the fountain – it's just the spray.' 'You silly girl!' exclaimed Magda. 'Do you not know how dangerous is it to sit by a wet fountain in such heat? My God. You will catch *la grippe* if you persist in this folly. Furthermore, damp clothes are very inelegant. Please do not do such a thing again. The damp is also bad for your hair,' she added, casting a critical eye at the same, and thinking, I wonder if I could persuade her to go to Raoul, he is the only person in this entire city or perhaps this entire country who could cut such hair. Ah, the people here know *nothing*. And this child here knows, my God, even less.

They had reached the Staff Entrance and Lisa ran up the fire stairs to change. Magda looked at her retreating figure and began her own slower and briefer ascent in a state of some satisfaction. She was doing arithmetic in her head and reassuring herself that, at the rate she and Stefan were going, they would by the end of the next year have saved enough capital to buy the lease of a shop in Macleay Street or even Double Bay: for Magda had every intention of presiding in time over her own extremely exclusive and exorbitantly expensive frock shop, and the Model Gowns could go to hell.

9

Patty Williams and Fay Baines were sitting at a table in the Staff Canteen at Goode's on the second Monday in December. They did not usually have their luncheon break at the same time, but with Lisa on the strength it was now felt to be a convenient arrangement as far as the manning of Ladies' Cocktail was concerned, because in fact this section tended not to be too busy during the lunch hour, Ladies, it seemed, who bought Cocktail Frocks preferring to do so earlier in the day or else, in a rush, much later. So here they were. But it was more convenient for Patty than for Fay as any intelligent person might have observed, for such a one would have noted that Fay's make-up today covered a very wan reality: her eyelids indicated sleeplessness and her pallor dejection.

'Is that a new face powder you're trying?' said Patty. 'It looks paler than your usual. I always use the same one, myself. Never changed since I left school. I don't suppose Frank'd notice even if I did,' she added, with a modulation of tone which promised worse. Here it came. 'I could paint my face green and he wouldn't notice, not him. Oh well.' And she pursed her lips, because she suddenly thought to herself, I don't want to be saying things like that to *Fay*. 'The trouble with Frank is,' she went on, more brightly, 'he's got this new boss who he doesn't get on with. He says he's too full of himself.' Ah yes, that was indeed the trouble: it was so much trouble that Frank had disburdened himself of no less than three whole sentences at the Williams steakfest on the previous Friday night, at the conclusion of his first week under the new regime in the Wonda Tiles Sales Department. 'The new boss is a slimy bastard,' said Frank. 'He thinks he owns the place. I don't know who he thinks he is.'

There was something more specific about his new chief which got on Frank's nerves and which he didn't mention to Patty at all, partly because he had not in fact properly acknowledged it to himself: it was something which irritated and in due course infuriated him without his being able to face it squarely and in its entirety: it was that the new boss had placed a large framed photograph of his two sons – a pair of grisly little tykes, eight and ten or thereabouts, Frank would have said if asked – on his desk: his desk at Wonda Tiles! And as soon as the opportunity had arisen, he'd pointed them out to his subordinates. 'Those are my two sons,' he had said, bursting with fatuous pride, 'Kevin and Brian.' And he grinned broadly. 'Eh, very nice,' said Frank's workmates. 'Oh, yeah,' said Frank. And then as if all this weren't quite bad enough, in the pub on Friday night the bastard had re-introduced the topic: and stone me if all the others hadn't joined in with remarks about their own sons and even their daughters. On it went. Suddenly everyone was boasting about their kiddies: and it was all the fault of this smarmy bastard of a new boss. Frank slunk off home to Randwick in a fine sulk, and when he played golf on the Saturday, his handicap went to hell.

'Well anyway,' said Patty, 'he doesn't like him. I don't know. We can't always have what we want, can we? He should try working under Miss Cartright for a week, I told him! Then he'd see.' And having thus returned the conversation to their common ground, she looked again at Fay. 'Is it the new powder or is it you?' she asked. 'You look a bit peaky. Are you feeling okay?' And an exciting and horrible notion sprang into her mind: could Fay be under the weather? *could Fay be pregnant?* She wasn't eating much: she had a salad in front of her which had hardly been touched. Fay looked up, slightly distractedly. Her deepest thoughts had been elsewhere. 'I'm fine,' she said. 'I was out late last night, that's all. Not enough sleep.' Oh, really, thought Patty.

Patty's speculations were as grotesque a version of reality as usual. The fact was that Fay had had a dislocating experience on Saturday night: she had been at a party given by one of Myra's cronies in a flat at Potts Point and she had suddenly, for no reason, become aware just before midnight that she was wasting her time: that she had in a sense met every one of the men there before, at every other party she had ever attended, and that she was tired of the whole futile merry-go-round: and what was worse than this, much, much worse, was that there was no other merry-go-round she could step onto: it was this one to which she was apparently condemned, whether she liked it or not, and suddenly now she did not, and there was not a damned thing she could do about it: try, try, try again, and die, she had thought despairingly, as she had travelled homewards in the back of someone's Holden. And despite all that she had met a man who'd been at the party for a few drinks at the Rex Hotel last night as she had agreed to do, and had spent another inglorious evening making conversation with Mr Wrong, and now, today, she felt entirely washed out, that was all. 'I just need a good night's sleep, that's all,' she told Patty.

'Yes, well,' said Patty, and she looked around the room, and she saw Paula Price, who she used to work with in Children's, who had done well for herself at Goode's, having now risen to a position of seniority in Ladies' Lingerie. 'If you can spare me,' she said to Fay, 'I'll just go over and chat to Paula; I haven't seen her for quite a while.'

The upshot of this chat was that Patty returned to her Ladies' Cocktail post via the Lingerie Department on the first floor, because Paula wanted her to see some *divine* nightdresses which had only just come in: an order which had arrived late but which Goode's had accepted nonetheless because the stock was so exceptional.

Made in a new improved kind of English nylon which, Paula assured Patty, *breathed*, the nightdresses came in three different styles, in three different colours, but for some reason – perhaps, simply, because the time had come – Patty, against all the odds, had fallen straightaway for one particular model out of all the permutations on offer. When Patty – thin, straw-coloured and unloved Patty – saw the black improved nylon nightdress with the gently gathered skirt edged in a black ruffle, its cross-over bodice and cap sleeves edged in black lace through which was threaded pale pink satin ribbon, her heart was lost, and without a second's hesitation her hand went, figuratively, into her pocket. 'Put it on lay-by for me,' she told Paula, 'and I'll settle up next pay-day.' Well, it wasn't all that dear, with the staff discount, after all, and she needed a new nightie; I mean, she thought, when did I last buy a nightie? And she looked at the swimming costumes as well, on the way back upstairs to Ladies' Cocktail, but she left that for another day: I don't want to go mad, she thought.

10

Fay Baines and her friend Myra Parker were sitting in a booth in Repin's eating toasted sandwiches, because they were going to a five o'clock, and since it would not finish until after their usual dinner time they ought to have, as Myra pointed out, some proper food to keep themselves going instead of ruining their figures by stuffing themselves with ice-creams and chocolates to stave off their hunger half-way through the film. This was the sort of forward-planning for which Myra was always to be trusted.

Myra's head was much better screwed down than Fay's; Myra had a knack for managing the affairs of life. She was now a hostess-cum-receptionist in a night club, with a considerable dress allowance, but she did not take advantage of Fay's discount privileges at Goode's, because the evening frocks at Goode's, she said, were not the type of thing. 'I need something more glamorous,' she told Fay. 'I'll try the Strand Arcade, or maybe the Piccadilly.'

It was the Saturday following that wan Monday when Fay had

sat in front of a salad in the canteen and made such a poor (but interesting) impression on Patty Williams, and she still wasn't looking her best even though she'd now clocked up several good nights' sleep. Myra poured herself a second cup of tea from the heavy little silver-plated teapot; she leaned back comfortably in her seat and lit a cigarette, and peered at Fay as she exhaled the smoke. 'Honey,' she said – Myra tended to meet quite a few Americans in the line of her duties – 'honey, I don't like the looks of you today: you don't look your usual lovely self. Is anything up?'

Fay looked at her plate. What could she say? 'It's probably just this new face powder,' she improvised, 'I think maybe it makes me look pale.' 'Then you'd better not use it,' said Myra; 'you don't want to look *pale*. You can use some of mine when we go to the Ladies': you want to look your best later on, don't you?' Myra smiled slyly, and blew out more smoke. She was referring to a dinner engagement with two men she had met at the night club. 'I'll bring my friend,' she had said when the date was suggested to her; 'she's game for anything – but a really nice girl: you needn't get any funny ideas, youse. Fay's a *nice* girl. And so am I, in case you hadn't noticed.' 'That's exactly why we want you to go out with us,' said the more extrovert of the two men, 'don't we, eh?' and he nudged his friend in the arm. 'Oh yeah, right you are!' said he. 'We'll meet you at the Cross, then, eight-thirty, at Lindy's,' said Myra. 'And don't keep us waiting.' 'As if we would,' they said. 'Eight-thirty sharp!'

Fay's heart sank. She had been meeting these men, or others resembling them in every important particular, throughout her adult life. She had eaten their dinners, drunk gin-and-limes at their expense, and she had danced in their arms; she had fought off, and sometimes submitted to, their love-making. She had travelled this particular road to its bitter and now dusty end and her heart now failed her, but to decline this evening's engagement had been a thing impossible: Myra would have thought she was mad. 'Gee, yes,' she told her friend. 'You never know, do you? He might be the one I've been waiting for. Is he tall?' Myra thought about the less attractive of the two men: the other she had bagged for herself. 'Not very,' she said, 'but he's not *short*. Just medium. Listen, though,' she added, quickly, 'I think he's rich. I think I remember seeing a gold watch on his wrist. I reckon you'll like him; I reckon he's your type. Wait and see!' 'Yes, okay,' said Fay, a tiny flicker of hope and courage stirring within her sad heart. 'I'll wait and see.' 'That's the stuff,' said Myra.

II

Lisa and her mother were going to the pictures this Saturday evening, too; it was what they usually did on Saturday evenings. Sometimes Lisa's father came with them; it depended. 'We'll wait and see whether your dad wants to come,' said Mrs Miles to her daughter about half an hour before he was due to come home from the races where he had spent the afternoon and God knew (Mrs Miles never would) how much of his salary. She wiped the working surfaces of the kitchen over once more with a sponge and rinsed it out. Lisa sat at the table. 'I hope that job isn't too much for you, Lesley,' said her mother, looking at her carefully. 'I was hoping to see you get a bit fatter, now your exams are over.' 'I'm all right, Mum,' said Lisa. 'I'm fine. I'll get fat in the New Year, after the job ends. I'll stay home all day and read, and get fat.' 'That's a good girl,' said Mrs Miles. 'I'll buy you some chocolate to eat, to help you along.' 'Oh thanks, Mum,' said Lisa.

Lisa and her mother had a secret which they had only shared by the fewest of words and looks: a secret and terrible plan had now begun to formulate itself whereby Lisa, should she actually gain the Commonwealth Scholarship which would pay her fees, would in fact, by one means or another and in defiance of her father's *ukase*, enter the University of Sydney in the new term. The secret occasionally became present in both their minds at once: it then seemed to hover above their heads in the form of a pink invisible cloud which glowed at its margins, too beautiful to indicate, too frail to name. It hovered now, as each imagined Lesley, Lisa, fatter, stronger, and an undergraduate. First, though, they must each – again secretly, in private and alone – suffer the agony of waiting for the examination results upon which all else depended. Three more weeks of this agony remained.

'There's your Dad now,' said Mrs Miles. 'Let's see what he wants to do.' The paterfamilias came into the kitchen. 'Hello there,' he said. He did not kiss them. He stood in the doorway, looking quite pleased with himself, as well he might: his pockets were full of five-pound notes. 'Did you have a good day, Ed?' asked Mrs Miles, meaning, did you enjoy the racing. 'Not bad, not bad,' said he, meaning, I won over a hundred quid, which begins to make up for the hundred and fifty I lost last week. 'Will you come out to the pictures with us tonight, Dad?' asked Lisa. 'We can see—' and she gave him an account of the alternative programmes which were showing in the neighbourhood. 'Oh well, I don't mind,' said Mr Miles expansively; 'I don't mind: you ladies choose. Maybe we'll have a Chinese meal beforehand: what do you reckon? Lesley can pay for it now she's working.' 'Get away with you,' said Mrs Miles. 'Lesley has to save that money. We'll eat at home. I've got some lovely lamb chops.' 'Keep your chops,' said Mr Miles. 'I'm only kidding. The treat's on me. Go and get yourselves ready both of you and let's be off.'

They ran to do his bidding, almost elated: these moods of good humour were rare enough to be entered into with as much alacrity as gratitude. Lisa put on her pink frock, and looking at herself in the full-length mirror in her mother's wardrobe thought to herself, it's not really – it's not quite – I wish – and realised that without her noticing it at the time, her two weeks at Goode's had somewhat altered her perception of the Good Frock. Oh well, she thought. I'm just going out with Mum and Dad, it's not as if – and now realised that all manner of possibilities had started lately to crowd her mind: all manner: that life really was, in all manner of possibilities, truly now and almost tangibly beginning.

12

Magda opened her great brown eyes to the dazzling day. She glanced at the bedside clock: it was ten o'clock: she wondered for a moment whether she would get up and go to Mass, and then she turned over and went back to sleep again. I need it more, she said to herself, God knows.

Magda had an entirely satisfactory understanding with God: this understanding was the foundation of her success in the art of living. Stefan had an entirely satisfactory understanding with himself, with the same consequences. That Magda and Stefan had an entirely satisfactory understanding with each other was the consequence of numerous determinants, such as the fact that they had each survived hell.

When Magda awoke again it was to the sight of Stefan standing over her with the coffee pot and a large cup and saucer. 'It occurs to me,' said he, 'that if I awaken you now – it is eleven a.m., by the way – you will have time to go to the Mass at midday. Should you so wish.' 'A-a-a-h,' Magda sighed, and stretched. 'First give me the coffee. Then I shall address the question.' She sat up, in a heave of white arms and satin nightdress, and Stefan poured out her coffee. 'I will fetch my own,' he said, leaving the room. Magda considered the day ahead. It would be pleasant to do nothing, and then to walk in a park, and to eat dinner in a restaurant with some friends. Stefan re-entered the room. 'I will not go to Mass today,' Magda told him. 'The Pope himself would excuse you,' said Stefan. 'Do not speak so of His Holiness,' said Magda, sternly.

Magda was Slovene and Stefan Hungarian; as Displaced Persons they had been given entry after the end of the war to the Commonwealth of Australia, and it was in a migrant camp outside Sydney that they had first laid eyes on each other. They had begun their life's conversation in French and as the efficient instruction provided by the Federal Government progressed, had switched over to English. Within a year of their arrival in Australia they were both fluent, however idiosyncratic, English-speakers and they then began also to read voraciously. Soon Stefan was branching into the classics but here Magda could but barely follow him. 'I cannot get along with this Shakespeare,' she said; 'this Hamlet prince, for example: he is not to me the stuff of heroes.' Their common language soon came to contain various old-fashioned locutions which, transferred from the pages of such as Hardy and Dickens, had found their way eventually via Stefan's into Magda's discourse, and even sometimes into that of their many Hungarian friends who in Magda's presence at least spoke English habitually. They all agreed sardonically that although the war – and more recently the revolution – and their own consequent fortunes had been a heavy price to pay for the privilege, they were and would remain grateful for the acquisition of 'this wonderful language' and they were still liable to laugh delightedly at a newly discovered idiom. 'A pig in a poke!' they might exclaim; and they would shout with pleasure, the way their Magyar ancestors might have done, as they rode their swift horses across the vast and fertile Hungarian plain.

13

At nine in the morning on the third Monday in December the great glass and mahogany doors of Goode's Department Store were opened to a large bevy of early-rising housewives all determined upon the prosecution of their Christmas shopping campaigns. From the wooded slopes of the salubrious North Shore to the stuccoed charm of the Eastern Suburbs, from the passé gentility of the Western ditto to the *terra incognita* of the Southern, had they travelled by train, bus, tram and even taxi cab to this scene of final frantic activity. There remained presents to be bought for sundry difficult relations, there remained clothes to be purchased for their gigantically-growing children, there remained even frocks to be found for themselves, and then shoes to match these frocks: there remained almost everything to play for, and they were resolved to win.

Miss Jacobs stood at her post, ready for anything whatsoever, her tape-measure draped around her neck and her pins beside her. Let them come: she would be as a rock in the great storm. Mr

Ryder walked past. 'Everything shipshape, Miss Jacobs?' he called. 'Ready for the fracas?' 'I don't know about any "*fracas*",' said Miss Jacobs to Lisa. 'We're bound to be very busy in the last week before Christmas, aren't we now? I don't know about any "*fracas*".' Christmas this year fell on the Tuesday of the following week. 'And mind you tell them, Lisa,' continued Miss Jacobs, 'that if they want alterations doing before Christmas, we can only do hems by then, not seams, and we can't do hems either after Wednesday, whatever they say. After Wednesday, with the holiday and everything, they can't have their alterations until the New Year.' 'Yes, I'll tell them,' said Lisa. 'And I'll just remind Miss Baines and Mrs Williams likewise,' said Miss Jacobs.

These were occupied with the display, Patty chattering to Fay about the deficiencies of her last-year's-model swimming costume as they had been revealed the day before on Coogee Beach. 'It's got elastic around here,' she said, drawing a line across part of her anatomy, 'but the elastic's going: and anyway it's faded. So I think I'll get a new one. Anyway you need two cossies, really. I need another one. I think I might get one of those satin lastex ones. I'll see. I'll spend my Christmas bonus on myself, for a change.' As if anyone had ever suggested she should do anything else. The coming Thursday was pay-day: she would have her fortnight's wages plus the bonus, and she would pay for her nightdress, and she might get a new swimming costume as well, and never mind the Bank of New South Wales. She had already bought all her Christmas presents. 'We're going to Mum for Christmas Day, all of us,' she told Fay, 'as per usual. What will you do?'

Ah, that was a sore point, even a sad one. There wasn't time to go down to Melbourne to her brother's, even if she wanted to: if Fay didn't accept Myra's invitation to go with her to Myra's parents, who had retired to the Blue Mountains where they lived in a little fibro cottage at Blackheath, then she would be quite alone, and this being unthinkable, she realised, but did not want to admit, that she was bound for Blackheath. 'It will be a nice break,' said Myra. 'We can stay till the Thursday morning and come back down on The Fish, you'll be back in plenty of time to start work.' It was the thought of The Fish which made the whole prospect tolerable to Fay's imagination: that legendary train: The Fish. 'I'm going to the Blue Mountains, with my girlfriend Myra,' she told Patty. 'I'll stay till Thursday morning and come back on The Fish.' 'Oh, that's nice,' said Patty, 'you'll be nice and cool.' And you could do with a break, she thought; you've been looking an absolute misery. So much for all those men you're always talking about. Perhaps she really is in trouble, she thought: hmm: oh well, it's none of my business.

Magda gave her black-clad sisters a further day to themselves, and then she struck. Early on Tuesday morning she emerged from her rosy cavern and sailed across the carpet to Ladies' Cocktail. 'Good morning, my ladies,' she cried, happily. 'I hope you are not too busy this week, for I am going to steal your little schoolgirl away for a while now and then. I have spoken to Miss Cartright and she says I may borrow your Lisa for a few mornings, a few afternoons; you will hardly notice.' Not much, you will, she thought, except that you will have to go to the stock-room yourselves and it will do you good too, instead of sending little Lisa every single time, and for every other errand requiring a pair of legs. 'Well,' said Miss Jacobs, 'if that's what Miss Cartright says, I'm not going to argue with you.' Patty looked offended, as she usually did in Magda's presence, and Fay looked askance. 'Shall I come now?' asked Lisa. 'That will be very kind,' said Magda. 'I will show you the way we do things in Model Gowns, there will be much for you to learn, and then we shall see.' Lisa slipped out from behind the counter which belonged to the Ladies' Cocktail section, and glancing and half-shrugging as if in apology to her colleagues followed Magda across the carpet and under the archway which marked the entrance to the shrine, and Miss Jacobs, Mrs Williams and Miss Baines saw her no more, until the sun had crossed the meridian, and twelve Cocktail Frocks had been sold, and three trips made to the stock-room, two by Miss Baines, and one by a much-complaining Mrs Williams.

14

'Well, Lisa,' said Magda, extending a graceful arm, 'here are the Model Gowns. Do you by the way know what is a Model Gown?' 'Well,' said Lisa, 'not exactly. I'm not sure—' 'Very well,' said Magda, 'I will explain to you. These frocks are all unique. There are no others like them in all this city. Oh, if you were to go to Focher perhaps you would find one or two, I don't know, that woman is capable of anything, but as far as we are concerned there can be no others of their kind in Sydney. A woman who buys one of these frocks knows that she will not meet another wearing the same frock, which is so terrible a thing to happen to a woman, even if she looks better in the frock than her rival. So to say. So we have the exclusive right to sell the frock in Sydney. You might find it at George's in Melbourne, that is all. Who goes to Melbourne? So that is by the way.' 'Yes,' said Lisa, bemused. 'I see.' 'And the stock is all here. We do not keep different sizes of the same model,' Magda continued, 'for then of course the frock would cease to be unique. Do you see?' And Lisa nodded, and gazed at the frocks, whose chiffon and taffeta edges frothed out in their luminous ranks around her. 'Now let us look perhaps at a few of these frocks,' said Magda, 'and you will see what such a Model Gown looks like. Let me see. We have our day frocks here and our costumes, as you would say I suppose our *suits*, here for instance this Irish linen, it is Hardy Amies, so very well cut, I would like it for myself but on the other hand I am not at my best in the English style, it is for a thin woman with no hips, I cannot understand why, English women are all made in the shape of a pear. Never mind. It is nothing to me. The French, they cut to fit a real woman with hips and a bosom, but they make her look slim nonetheless: *that* is artistry. There is no one to touch them, my God, it is a remarkable civilisation. I hope you have learnt some French at your school, have you?' 'Yes, oh yes,' said Lisa, 'I took French for the Leaving Certificate.' '*C'est bien*,' said Magda. '*Nous parlerons quelquefois français, non?*' '*Je lis un peu*,' said Lisa, '*je ne park pas bien.*'

'You will come and see some French evening frocks, *en tout cas*,' said Magda, 'which will interest you I dare say more than the costumes or the day frocks. For a *jeune fille*, the romantic. And we have some English ones too of course, they are not bad, see what you think. Here is Hartnell, he is the dressmaker of the Queen as you know, Amies again, also he makes for the Queen, and a Charles James – *magnifique*. Now some French, you see – Jacques Fath, *ravissante*, a little Chanel, she has such wit that woman, and the great Dior. Who can touch him.'

Lisa stared, more bemused than ever; her head began to swim. She had lately come to see that clothing might be something beyond a more or less fashionable covering: that it might have other meanings: what she now but dimly and very oddly, very suddenly, saw was a meaning she could not before have suspected: what she now but dimly, oddly, and so suddenly, saw was that clothing might be – so to speak – art: for these frocks, as each was named and held out briefly before her gaze by Magda, seemed each to exist in a magical envelope of self-sufficiency, or even a sort of pride; each of these frocks appeared to her however ignorant still lively intelligence to be like – it was astonishing – a poem. 'Gosh,' she said; 'golly.' Her hand reached out, gently, tentatively, and she touched the many-layered skirt of a pale evening frock. 'Are they very expensive?' she asked, her eyes large and fearful. 'Ho!' snorted Magda. 'Ha! they had better be expensive. My God! You will see my stock-book very soon and then you will know. But with such a frock, the price as you may one day appreciate is part of the charm. Now I will tell you something else, one or two things, and then you had better go back to those Cocktail ladies, and later I will speak to Miss Cartright again and will suggest to her that you will come to me in the mornings, when it is not so busy here, to help me with something I am going to explain.' And she led the way to the Louis XVI table and pulled out the drawer. '*Voilà!*' she said; 'here then is my stock-book. Now then. As you know, the abominable sales will begin on the second of January and I too must put my stock on sale. So it is time to review it. Now you see: here are listed every one of my frocks, their names, their wholesale and their retail prices, and you will be most kind to make out a little ticket for each one which is not sold yet – you see we make a tick in the last column here when a frock is sold – with the price on it, and when all that is done, we will go through the stock and I will decide on the sale price depending on how long the frock has been here and its condition and so on. Then you will write the sale price beneath the old price so that the ladies know they get a great great bargain. And first of all you will arrange all the frocks of each section in the same order as that in the stock-book, you see, which will be more convenient, we will know where we are. And of course you will always make sure that your hands are quite quite clean before you come in here and touch these so-expensive frocks, *ma petite*. Okay?' And she smiled brightly, thinking to herself that it was very nice to have a little assistant, even a thin pale little schoolgirl like Lisa, who knew nothing; in fact, it was very nice to have the charge of so ignorant a little girl, for she, Magda, could teach her everything, and suddenly now, she, Magda, realised how pleasant it was to give instruction, to fill an empty head with knowledge, drop by precious drop: cut, style, taste; Amies, Fath, Dior.

15

'I'm going to help Magda in the mornings, Mum.' 'Magda? Who's "Magda"?' asked Mrs Miles. 'You know, Magda. She's in charge of Model Gowns; I told you.' 'Model Gowns? Now what's "model gowns" for goodness' sake?' asked Mrs Miles. 'I thought they were all "model gowns" at Goode's. An expensive shop like that.' 'No, no,' said Lisa. 'They're just un-model gowns, all the other things in Goode's, they come in all sizes, anyone can buy them.' 'Anyone who can pay for them,' said Mrs Miles. 'I'm sure I can't.' 'No, but—' continued Lisa, 'the Model Gowns are unique. There's only one of each, and they're from France and England, and if you have one, you know nobody else will have it too, because it's the only one in Sydney.' 'Oh, yes,' said Mrs Miles, 'I know. Individual. Well, no one else has the same clothes as you do either, except for your old school blouses, because I make them, so they're unique too, aren't they?' 'Ye-e-es,' said Lisa, 'yes, I suppose so—' 'Well, there's no "suppose" about it,' said her mother; 'they *are*. That pink frock I made you, if you could get one like it I reckon you'd pay five or six pounds at least, but you can't.' 'Yes, but the Model Gowns,' said Lisa, 'are mostly evening frocks.' 'Oh, yes, evening frocks; I see,' said Mrs Miles. 'For balls, and that. That's another story. I suppose I could try my hand at that if you wanted to go to a ball.' And she began to get a dizzy feeling at the thought of making an evening frock, for a ball, not that she wouldn't do her best, not that she wouldn't try her very best to dress her daughter for a ball. Well. 'But then you haven't reached that point yet so we needn't worry about it yet, need we?' she asked brightly: but while she was doing so, each naturally had the same awful thought: the secret suddenly rose in a pink cloud and hovered near the kitchen ceiling above their heads. If Lesley is really going to go to the university, thought Mrs Miles, she'll very likely be going to balls, she'll be doing goodness knows what: the clothes! All those other girls there – the daughters of professional men, business men: rich girls, with lots of clothes, clothes from Goode's, for example – it was going to be a headache, keeping up with that. Lesley had been such a slow developer, her life had been so simple, so far – she had hardly been out with a boy: only a few young chaps she called weeds, chaps she didn't care about making an impression on: how would it be when she got to the university, and met others, not weeds – well. She would just have to do her best. They would see. 'No, but when I do go to a ball,' said Lisa, 'I'll have my money I've saved working at Goode's, won't I? So I can buy something, and not bother you about it.' 'That's true,' said her mother; 'I'd forgotten that. You could buy a model gown, with that money. You'll look just lovely.' They laughed together, and Lisa jumped up and took her mother's arm and they danced around the room, singing together.

Volare, oh, oh!
Cantare, oh, oh, oh, oh!

Everything will work out somehow, thought Mrs Miles; and my Lesley will go to the ball.

16

It was on the morning of the very next day that Lisa saw The Frock.

She was engaged upon the task which Magda had described to her, checking the stock-list against the actual frocks and ranging these in the order in which they appeared in the stock-list so that Magda could later go through them speedily and decide upon their sale prices. She had managed to find and to arrange in the correct order five or six of the semi-formal evening frocks which hung together in one mahogany open cabinet on their pink satin-covered hangers and was now hunting amongst the unsorted remainder for the model named 'Tara', described in the book as black and white silk taffeta, Creed. As she carefully slid each hanger forward to inspect the Model Gown which hung behind it, finding now 'Laura', now 'Rosy', now 'Minuit', but never yet 'Tara', her gaze was suddenly – as she pushed 'Minuit' further forward to clear a space – filled with the vision of – it was a magical coincidence – 'Lisette'.

Child of the imagination of a great *couturière*, having that precise mixture of the insouciant and the romantic, the sophisticated and the simple, that only the female mind can engender, 'Lisette' was the quintessential evening frock for a young girl: a froth of red pin-spotted white organza with a low neck, a tight bodice, a few deep ruffles over the shoulders, artful red silk piping edging these ruffles and the three tiers of the gathered skirts whose deepest tier would have cleared the floor by some eight inches, to leave a good view of a slender leg, a delicate ankle. The effect was of tiny spots set off by narrow stripes, the gaiety of crimson set off by the candour of white; the silky fabric very faintly shimmered. Lisa stood, gazing her fill. She was experiencing for the first time that particular species of love-at-first-sight which usually comes to a woman much earlier in her life, but which sooner or later comes to all: the sudden recognition that a particular frock is not merely pretty, would not merely suit one, but answers beyond these necessary attributes to one's deepest notions of oneself. It was her frock: it had been made, however unwittingly, for her. She stood for a long time, drinking it in. The encounter was faintly, vaguely, strangely similar to her first meeting with the Tyger. She gazed on, marvelling, and then at last slowly, wrenchingly, she pushed the hanger forward, and continued her search for 'Tara'.

17

Miss Jacobs, Mrs Williams, Miss Baines and Miss Miles had just received their wages envelopes, with their Christmas bonuses added on, which aroused very satisfactory sensations in each one as she contemplated the disposition of the surplus funds. The shape of Miss Jacobs's contemplations must remain forever a mystery; Lisa's we might quite easily guess at; Fay's perhaps less easily; Patty's, we know. 'I'm just going to change out of this black frock,' she told Fay at lunchtime, 'and go down and look at them swimming cossies, and one or two other things maybe, so maybe I'll see you in the canteen later on, and maybe not, I might have to skip lunch today.' Oddly for her she had not mentioned the black nightdress to a soul: it was her secret. Except for Paula, of course. She would just change now very quickly and then run down to Lingerie and – no, she thought, I won't; I'll go to the cossies first, because I don't want anyone to see me carrying that parcel from Lingerie (which used a different patterned wrapping paper, printed with a lace and ribbon design) because they might guess what's in it, or they might ask. So I'll just go to the cossies first.

The consequence was that she spent so much time trying on swimming costumes and then suddenly felt so hungry that she thought, I haven't time to get my nightie and eat as well so I'll get my nightie tomorrow; and that was how she came at last to reach home on the Friday night before Christmas carrying a Goode's Lingerie parcel containing one black nylon nightdress with pink satin ribbon trim, SSW.

The sun had shone constantly every day now for several weeks during which the temperature had steadily, relentlessly, risen, and every wall in the vast city, every pavement, every roof, was soaked in heat. People moved slowly through the miasmic atmosphere, their eyes narrowed against the glare; their minds contracted into a state of wilting apathy, they directed their slow steps as soon as they could towards water in whatever form they could most conveniently find it: they went to the beaches, the swimming baths, their own showers, and immersed themselves until at last the stupendous sun sank below the horizon and darkness laid its balm upon their assaulted senses. Patty reached Randwick on the Friday night before Christmas just as this benison began to fall.

I wonder how long I've got before Frank gets in, she thought; he'll be having a proper booze-up as it's Friday night so he probably won't get home till sevenish: so I've got time for a good long soak. And she took off all her sticky clothes and went into the bathroom, and turned on the shower. Standing under its downpour, she drifted into that primeval condition, a state of peacefulness suffused by an innocent sensuality, which immersion in water can alone induce, and it was fully fifteen minutes before she turned off the taps. She had washed her hair: her permanent wave was almost grown out and it hung in limp strands around her small face. As she re-entered the bedroom her eye lit upon the secretive package which contained her new nightdress and she thought: I know: I'll try it on now, and just see what it looks like *on*. And she did.

She stood for some time gazing at herself in the full-length mirror in the wardrobe door, for she could not quite believe in the reality of the sight which met her eyes. Geez, she exclaimed to herself: geez-uz.

I'll be damned, thought Frank, if I'll go to the pub with them lot tonight, and listen to any more bull about their flaming kids. The topic was getting out of hand: some of the mates had even started producing – not half sheepishly enough, either –snapshots of their own: 'Here's my Cheryl – curly hair, see? She gets it from me—' Frank was damned if he wanted to listen to any more of that, and in the pub, too. So tonight he sulked off – 'Things to do. See youse on Monday!' And he went, without even thinking twice, to another pub on the other side of Central Railway Station, a little place he'd half noticed long ago, and he went into the public bar, and he asked for some whisky. I feel like a whisky, he thought; I just feel like a whisky. 'Scotch or Australian?' asked the barmaid. Well, there's no need to go completely cuckoo, thought Frank. 'Australian's good enough for me,' he told the barmaid. 'Right you are,' she said, and she poured him a measure of Australian whisky. Used as he was to drinking beer, Frank tossed it off. 'Same again!' he said. After some time he walked out into the street and found his way to his tram stop; it was a toast-rack tram on that route, and he wobbled slightly all the way home in a haze of whisky and unarticulated anguish. I wonder what's for dinner, he thought.

Patty had her back to the bedroom door and had only half heard Frank's key turning in the lock: that will be Frank, she dimly thought, I'd better make myself look decent: and she opened the wardrobe door – her still-unfamiliar transparent-black-clad reflection coming up close to meet her – to find her dressing-gown. As she did so, she suddenly saw, beyond her reflection, the figure of her husband, standing in the doorway of the bedroom. 'What are you doing in here?' he asked. 'I'm just – I'm just getting my dressing-gown,' said Patty. 'Dressed for bed?' asked Frank, taking in Patty's apparel now quite precisely. 'Isn't it a bit early for that?' 'Well, not really,' said Patty. 'It's new. I was just trying it on. I'll take it off now.' '*I'll* take it off,' said Frank. And he came over to Patty, who had turned away from the wardrobe and her reflection, and stood in front of her for a few seconds, and then very gingerly he put his arms around her waist, and seizing in each hand a fold of the black nylon nightdress began to pull the garment up and over his wife's damp head. Patty could smell the whisky faintly on his breath, but she said nothing. Frank flung the nightdress aside and touched Patty's breast. He inclined his head ever so slightly towards the bed and Patty moved tentatively towards it. 'I reckon I'll take my clothes off too,' he said.

18

'I think I will ask little Lisa to come to luncheon here tomorrow after we finish at the shop,' said Magda to Stefan. 'What do you think? Would you enjoy meeting a little Australian schoolgirl? A bluestocking who has neither style nor beauty but who is charming, so well brought up, and so to say adorable in her naïveté.' 'What are you up to, my Magda?' asked her husband. 'What are you plotting in your Balkan brain? When have you developed this taste for little schoolgirls? Especially when you tell me she is not pretty, eh?' 'I did not say she is not pretty – though as a matter of fact she is not – I said she is not beautiful. You know perfectly well the difference. I would not like her more if she were pretty, but in fact she *will* be pretty: for I shall make her so. Anyone young can be pretty, with a little contrivance if needs be, and anyone young *should* be. It is otherwise a disaster, to be young, or at least a waste of time.' 'Ah, so you are going to turn a sow's ear into a silk purse, are you?' And Stefan laughed heartily. 'You may laugh – go on, laugh like a drain –' Stefan laughed the more – 'but I cannot see what is so funny. I do a good deed for once in my life, I cannot see the humour.' 'No, if you could, it would cease to be,' said Stefan, chuckling. 'Well, Magda my beauty, have your little schoolgirl here if they who have so well brought her up will permit such a thing – which I doubt – and I assure you you will have my full support; you know I am in favour of any enterprise which has beauty as its end.' 'I did not say I would make her beautiful,' said Magda, 'I said pretty. Please do not make me to be more of a fool than I am.' 'You are not at all a fool,' said Stefan. 'I will remember that you said pretty. Perhaps I would rather meet her *after* you have made her pretty, however.' 'Don't be silly,' said Magda. And supposing she can come, will you go up to the good delicatessen at Cremorne Junction tomorrow morning and buy some nice things for us to eat? Get some rye bread, also some black, some cream cheese if it is very fresh, some good ham—' Stefan cut her off. 'I can do the shopping,' he said, 'without a list, my angel. Oh but!' and he suddenly struck his head with one large hand, 'we are forgetting! Rudi comes tomorrow!' 'Ah yes,' said Magda. 'But we do not know when. He will quite possibly come much later – who can ever say, with Rudi? It does not matter in any case. What is one Hungarian the more or less? We will eat, we will talk; if Rudi is abominable Lisa and I will go out for a walk; everything will manage itself.'

Rudi was a comparatively recent – a post-revolution – emigrant, the cousin of the wife of one of Stefan's former clients: Stefan being an accountant with a small but thriving practice among the migrant colony of Sydney. The former client – Rudi's cousin-in-law – having moved to Melbourne a few years before, Rudi had tried life in that capital in the first instance, but having soon concluded that Sydney must be more to his taste was now about to launch himself on its brilliant blue expanses. 'I have had Melbourne,' he had announced at the end of three months in that place, 'up to here,' indicating as he did so a point roughly twelve inches above his head. Magda and Stefan had met him several times during his reconnaissance trip to Sydney: now that he had come lock stock and barrel to live there they had undertaken to introduce him to the crowd, help him find a flat, and generally give any necessary moral support. It did not appear that this latter would be much required.

The matter of his employment had already been settled, at least for the time being: he was to work for the cousin-in-law's former partner in the latter's import-export business. 'The work will be dull,' said the former partner, 'and poorly paid, but there is a wonderful view of Darling Harbour from the window of my office, and I give you leave to come and look at it as often as you please, up to a maximum of five minutes per *diem*.' 'Could anyone, I least of all, resist so handsome an offer?' said Rudi. 'Expect me on the first day of the New Year.' 'Better make that the second,' said his employer-to-be; 'the first is here a public holiday, and I would be breaking the law if I had you to work that day.' 'Unless you paid me time and a half,' said Rudi. 'Just so,' said his cicerone. 'So I will see you on the second, at nine a.m. sharp.'

19

Fay, leaving Goode's by the Staff Entrance on the Friday night before Christmas with her enlarged pay-packet in her handbag thought, I should buy something new to wear, it might cheer me up. She felt a dreadful lassitude which might, she thought, be merely the heat; but she could not remember the heat's having so affected her before. I'm just a bit down in the dumps, she told herself. I'll feel better after Christmas is over. And she caught herself thinking of Christmas as a trial, and she thought, what is the matter with me? And she tried to think of the Christmas before her as a pleasure, as something to look forward to – with Myra's parents, and Myra's brother and sister and their families all driving up from Penrith the one lot and Kurrajong the other – which was partly why the Parkers had decided on the Blue Mountains as a retirement home, to be near the grandchildren – on Christmas Day itself, and she thought oh well, safety in numbers. And she cheered herself up a little more, by thinking of the trip back on The Fish. I should buy a new dress to wear on Christmas

Day, she thought. That might cheer me up. But she wouldn't really have time to have a good look around: I'll skip it, she thought. I'll save my money for the sales. The blue and white will do. That's only last season's.

Fay had done a remarkable thing: she had cried off all proposed engagements this weekend (the gold watch had asked her out, I know he only wants one thing, she had told Myra, and Myra herself had wanted her to go to a party) and she was going to do absolutely nothing: she was going to stay at home, do all her washing, clean the flat, and wash and set her hair. She was going to read *The Women's Weekly* and if she finished that, she could read a book. She had the book with her now: Lisa had lent it to her. Lisa had been reading it in the canteen, and Fay had said, is that a good book? And Lisa had said yes, it's wonderful. I'm just finishing it. Would you like to borrow it? Well, okay, said Fay, to be polite. What's it called? It's called *Anna Karenina*, said Lisa, holding it up so that Fay could see the title printed on the cover.

20

'Lisa,' said Fay, 'I think Magda wants to speak to you.' Magda had indeed been making eloquent signals with her great eyes across the several yards of space which separated Model Gowns from Ladies' Cocktail. Lisa looked across the chasm and Magda beckoned; the girl hurried across to her. Had she not completed her allotted task the day before? She did not like to think of the frost which would settle on Mrs Williams if not also Miss Jacobs and even Miss Baines were she to abandon them once more on this busiest of all mornings. 'Lisa, my dear,' said Magda, 'I will not long detain you: I merely wish to invite you to luncheon today if you have nothing more amusing to do. I have so much described you to my husband who looks forward to meeting you, it will be very simple, we do not trouble with the *haute cuisine* on a Saturday – psssht! – it is the end of a long week – a piece of sausage, a glass of wine, a few cherries – please give us the pleasure of your company!'

Lisa was overwhelmed; she stuttered. 'I'll have to ask my

mother,' she said; 'I mean, I'll have to tell her.' 'But *naturally*!' cried Magda. 'I have thought of that too! Here are four pennies, I keep some always in my bureau in case of need – run quickly to the public telephones there and call your mother and ask her permission, please. You know we live in Mosman, it will be quite easy for you to find your way home, no? It is not so far. Go quickly, they will not notice, the ladies, and tell me what your mother says. And give her first my respects, please.'

Fay watched, unable to hear, and wondered. That Magda: how intriguing she was, as well as frightful: but Lisa did not seem to find her frightful: fearsome, possibly, but not frightful. Lisa seemed to enjoy her time at Magda's side: she would return from her stints at Model Gowns in a state of something like elation. 'There are frocks from Paris in there,' she had told them, 'and London: beautiful, the most beautiful frocks – you should go and see. Magda won't mind.' As if they would go and see! 'I don't want to see frocks from *Paris* and *London*,' said Patty Williams. 'I've got enough to do with frocks from *Sydney* and *Melbourne*.' But Fay, silenced by this remark, thought to herself, geez. I'd love to look at those frocks. And perhaps I will, later; or some time. She thought, perhaps they look like the frocks in magazines: geez, think of that: fancy having a frock that was in a magazine.

'We will jump onto a tram in Elizabeth Street and go quickly to the Quay,' said Magda to Lisa as they walked forth from Goode's at 12.35: 'I am in no mood for a promenade. Come.' Lisa had rarely had the occasion to travel by ferry and had entirely forgotten, if she had ever really known, the ravishing delight of the experience. 'We will sit outside, of course,' said Magda, running up the staircase and going out onto the upper deck, 'here, with our backs to the sun. Ouf! what could be more glorious?' She looked around at the Harbour, the sky, the Bridge, Pinchgut, the fairyland foreshores; the entire glittering panorama. Intoxicated by this spectacle and by the mad throbbing of the great engine and the strange allure of the smell of its oil, carried across the twinkling water on this comfortable wooden vessel with its cargo of fortunate passengers, the salty breeze in her hair, Lisa felt herself to be no longer on the threshold, but suddenly projected wholly into real life; to have left – at last – Lesley, that child, far behind. 'Isn't it lovely!' she exclaimed. 'Isn't it glorious! I *am* happy!' Magda turned and smiled at her brilliantly. 'Good!' she said. 'Be happy – always!' And she kissed Lisa on the cheek. Lisa smiled shyly at her. I've heard, she thought, that Continentals kiss each other much more than we do: it means nothing. They do it all the time: even the men. The men even kiss each other. But how strange I feel.

21

'Here we are at last!' exclaimed Magda, opening her front door; the remark might have been made for either Lisa's benefit, or Stefan's.

Lisa after a short walk up from the wharf now found herself entering a flat which occupied the upper floor of a sprawling Edwardian villa overlooking Mosman Bay. Light streamed through its great windows filling the large sitting room into which the door immediately opened; to the left could be seen a glimpse of kitchen, to the right, a half-open door revealed a small triangle of what might be a bedroom. Near to the kitchen she now saw a large round table covered with food, and standing next to it, a tall man with dark wavy hair and bright hazel eyes. This man was smiling at them broadly, and waved a hand over the table. 'See what I have conjured up for you,' he said, 'by the exercise of my great powers!' 'Never mind your great powers,' said Magda, 'come here and meet Lisa. Lisa, may I present my husband, Stefan Szombathelyi, who is a Hungarian but not, alas, a count. But you can't have everything.' Stefan, smiling at Lisa, drew himself up to his full height, clicked his heels, and bowed, taking Lisa's hand the while which he then kissed. 'I am enchanted to meet you,' he told her. He released her hand: she was not perhaps blushing, but she seemed rather pink. 'You must not mind, Lisa,' said Magda; 'I suppose you have heard that we Europeans are kissing people all the time.' They all laughed, but Lisa most especially.

'Now I will merely divest myself of this dreadful black,' said Magda, 'and we can eat. I am ravenous I must tell you. Excuse me very briefly. Stefan, give Lisa a glass of wine, please.' Stefan smiled nicely at the girl. She wasn't too bad: not pretty, but perhaps she had possibilities. She was very thin, but that was certainly better than being very fat. 'Would you like some wine?' he asked, 'or would you prefer lemonade? I have bought some, just in case. Such an amusing drink, don't you agree? But the wine is quite amusing too in its way. Tell me what you would like.' 'I think,' said Lisa, 'I'd like some lemonade. I don't usually drink wine.' She had not in fact drunk so much as a drop of this liquid ever in her life. 'Excellent,' said Stefan. 'I will fetch the lemonade, it is in the fridge. It is not amusing in the least when it is not cold.'

Magda re-entered the room as he departed; she was now clad in a becoming pair of red linen trousers. 'Now for some food,' she cried, rubbing her hands together as she approached the table. 'What has he bought for us? Come Lisa and sit, and help yourself please. I will cut some bread. Do you like rye bread? This is very good. Then you have what you like with it, cheese – various kinds all here on this plate, ham, yes, liverwurst, that sausage there is good or try this salami, then I see he has made us a salad as well – you must eat some of that, it is good for you. Stefan, pour me a glass of wine, I beg you.'

Lisa, dazed by the exotic goodies set before her, began to help herself to minute quantities of this and that. No such food had ever before come her way, and she might happily have tasted each thing slowly and in private, but soon she was distracted from any such whole-hearted gluttony by her host. 'Magda tells me you have just left school, Lisa,' said Stefan. 'Yes, I've just sat the Leaving Certificate,' said Lisa. 'Ah,' exclaimed Stefan, 'the Leaving! So you are clever!' 'I don't know yet,' said Lisa; 'I'm still waiting for the results.' 'That is a clever answer,' said Stefan, 'so I think you may wait with some confidence. When will you have them?' 'They come out in about three weeks' time,' said Lisa. 'And then?' said Stefan. 'Will you go to the university?' 'O-o-oh – I really don't know,' said Lisa, dreading at the contemplation of this question the possibility of not doing so. 'I'm trying not to think about it until I know.' 'This is quite correct,' said Magda. 'Do not make her think of imponderables, Stefan. She has plenty to think of straightaway. She has her job, she has still Christmas and the abominable sales before her, she lives in the moment.' 'To be sure,' said Stefan, 'so tell me: do you like to read novels, Lisa?' 'Oh *yes*,' said she. 'And what are you reading now?' he asked. 'I've just finished *Anna Karenina*,' said Lisa. 'I can't decide what to read next: there are so many to choose from.' 'How true,' said Stefan; 'and the number always grows, I assure you. It is a strange thing. But how did you like *Anna*?' 'Oh, I loved it. It's wonderful,' said Lisa. 'I agree that it is hard to think of what should follow it,' said Stefan. 'Perhaps it should be something quite different. Read about another woman: perhaps *Emma*. Have you read that yet?' 'No, I haven't.' 'Oh well that is settled then,' said Stefan. 'Jane Austen, I assure you, is as great a genius as Tolstoy, whatever they say. Let me have your opinion in due course.' Lisa smiled happily. No one had talked to her in this fashion before. 'Yes, I will,' she replied.

Magda now broke in. 'Have we no dessert?' she asked. 'Is there no fruit?' 'Yes, I will get it,' said Stefan. 'And put on the coffee,' said Magda. 'That too,' he replied. He went to the kitchen and returned with a pineapple. Ah, but this will be messy,' said Magda; 'do you mind, Lisa? Tuck your serviette under your chin, at any rate; the juice goes everywhere.' Stefan carved the pineapple and as they all sat munching and dribbling companionably, the doorbell rang. Magda looked up, her great eyes wide. 'That will be Rudi,' she exclaimed. 'He has such a sense of timing, like no one.'

22

Stefan opened the door and admitted the newcomer, and Lisa, turning, beheld a wiry and very handsome man of around thirty-five years of age. 'Stefan, my old bean,' cried he, 'and Magda my young bean – but I hope I am not late. Or early! How are you both? I have brought you a cake.' He handed a large flat box to Magda, and kissed her on both cheeks.

'Now that is very nice,' said Magda, 'we are just wanting cake here, for the coffee must be ready. Have you had lunch, Rudi? There is plenty here left over. But forgive me, Lisa. Let me introduce Rudi Jánosi, who has just come to Sydney to live, though we don't yet know precisely where. Rudi, this is my colleague Lisa Miles.' 'How do you do,' said Rudi politely. 'Sit down here and eat if you wish,' said Magda. 'No, I have had a snack,' said Rudi. 'Then we will be comfortable over here,' said Magda. 'If you have finished with the pineapple, Lisa, let us sit on the sofa and have our coffee and some cake. Sit, sit everyone, ouf! I must have a cigarette above all.'

She opened a silver box and took a cigarette from it; Stefan, having entered with the coffee pot and some cups on a tray, set it down and lit Magda's cigarette. 'So Rudi,' he said, 'we have been discussing Jane Austen. Tell us what you think of her.' 'My opinion has yet to be formed,' said Rudi; 'I have read not one word.' 'Ah, a philistine,' said Stefan. 'I have always wanted to meet one.' 'No, the truth is,' said Rudi, 'I am rather infatuated with Charles Dickens. Such horror! Such humour! You see, he is so much better in English than in Hungarian, so I am reading all over again what I read before so long ago. It is very amusing.' 'Dickens in Serbo-Croat I never read,' said Magda; 'I suppose there is such a thing. In English, however, his books remain at any rate stupendously long. I have not the time.' 'Magda prefers *Vogue*,' said Stefan. 'And Agatha Christie too,' Magda added. 'Tell us, Rudi, whether you have found a flat, or not?'

'I have looked at several, but the chief problem is to decide between this side of the Harbour or the other. It is difficult when I don't know where my girlfriend lives.' 'Which girlfriend is this?' asked Magda. 'Well, as you see I have not yet met her,' said Rudi, 'but I very soon shall, and I would rather not live on the opposite side of the Harbour. That would be stupid, a waste of time. So you see the difficulty.' 'In that case the sooner you meet her the better,' said Stefan; 'you cannot stay *chez* Benedek indefinitely.' 'Perhaps we should have a party,' said Magda. 'New Year's Eve. I have toyed with the idea. What do you think, Stefan?' 'Oh certainly,' said Stefan; 'anything to accommodate Rudi with a girlfriend, therefore a flat – let us have a party.' 'Not that we know so many girls,' said Magda. 'I will have to rack my brains. Lisa here is of course not only too young but too clever and too nice for you. But I hope she will come to the party nevertheless, if she is permitted.' Lisa looked eager. 'Oh, I'd love to,' she said. 'Do you like parties?' asked Rudi. 'I hope you will dance once at least with me, even if I am too old, too stupid and not nice enough.' Lisa laughed and agreed. Oh, she thought, this was real life! 'We have forgotten the cake!' cried Magda. 'Let us eat it, now.'

'Give me your opinion of the cake, anyway,' said Rudi to Lisa. 'I must say that in Melbourne, where I have been living so miserably, there are at least many better cakeshops than here.' 'In Melbourne they have more need of cake,' said Stefan, 'having more or less nothing else.' 'This is true,' said Rudi. 'It is a sad town, not by the way a city as they choose to pretend, not that they can know the difference. Sydney at any rate is undoubtedly a city, whereas Melbourne – well, there are of course some serious paintings in the Gallery, but nothing whatsoever more which pertains to a city; except of course for the cake.' 'Meanwhile here not only is the cake inferior,' said Stefan, 'but the Art Gallery is a joke.' 'Yes, but a joke in the most exquisite taste,' said Rudi. 'Do you not agree, Lisa?' 'I've never been there,' she replied. 'You see my point,' said Rudi to Stefan. 'You might come there with me one day,' said Rudi, 'if you will do me the honour. It is certainly worth at least one visit.'

Magda now decided that Lisa's head had been sufficiently turned by Rudi's facile gallantries and jumped to her feet. 'Come Lisa,' she said, 'let us leave these two to talk Hungarian together, poor things, and we will go for a walk which is advisable after all this cake, and then I must not keep you so long from your mother. We will first tidy ourselves a little. Come.' And she led the way into the bedroom.

She sat down at a large old-fashioned looking dressing table with a triple mirror, and Lisa stood uncertainly behind her. 'Sit here,' said Magda, making room on the wide low stool, 'there is plenty of room for us both. Use this comb, it is quite clean.' Lisa began to comb her hair. 'You know,' said Magda, 'I wonder how it would look to have the parting *here*', and she took the comb.

'But take off your glasses, they are a little in my way.' Lisa sat submissively, her glasses in her hand, while Magda drew a parting much farther to the side of her narrow forehead and combed out her hair. 'I think that is extremely nice!' said Magda. 'Look!' and Lisa stared into the mirror. 'Can you see without your glasses?' asked Magda. 'Oh yes, I only need them really for reading,' said Lisa. 'Then why wear them always?' asked Magda. 'I suppose because I am always reading,' said Lisa. 'Well, we must find something else for you to do,' said Magda. 'In the meantime leave them off, it is a novelty for you. Look now and see how you like yourself.' Lisa looked. It was a strange but interesting sight; she smiled with embarrassment. 'A little lipstick I think,' said Magda, opening a drawer and rummaging, 'your own has all worn off and you may like a different colour.' For your own is not a good one, she thought to herself. 'Here now,' she said, 'try this. A nice pink, suitable for a *jeune fille*. I cannot think what it is doing here, it is not the colour for me.' Lisa applied the lipstick. 'Blot it,' commanded Magda, giving her a tissue. She threw the tissue into a waste-basket and looked at Lisa's reflection. 'We will experiment with the eye make-up another time perhaps,' she said. 'Your eyes are nice, an interesting colour.' Lisa's eyes could now easily be seen, their irises a greyish shade of blue, the whites nice and clear. 'Stand back there,' said Magda, waving her hand towards the bed, 'and let me see the whole effect. Hmmm.' Lisa was wearing one of her gathered skirts and a white lawn blouse. Her face certainly now looked both more alert and better defined. 'You have so slim a figure,' said Magda, 'I envy you this so much: you might as well make the most of it and wear always a belt. I have so many – fat as I am – I may have something there you could wear. Have a look inside the door of that wardrobe. Go on, open it, there is no skeleton inside.' Lisa opened the door and saw hanging from a rail a dozen or so belts. Magda watched her. 'Try that tan leather,' she said, 'it will match your sandals.' Lisa took the belt and put it on. 'Tighter,' said Magda; 'use the last hole.' 'I have,' said Lisa. 'We will make another then,' said Magda. 'Come here.' She fished around and found a pair of nail scissors, and made another hole. 'Now then,' she said.

The belt, which was of course of superior quality, made the whole difference to Lisa's appearance. '*Ça va*,' said Magda, '*très bien*. I do not wear this belt often – you might as well keep it. It looks much better on you in any case. How wonderful, to have a twenty-two inch waist. And keep the lipstick also: it is the right colour for you. Throw away the other, nothing is more demoralising than a wrong colour. You look charming, with a bit more experience you will look enchanting; one needs all the weapons at one's command to deal with the Rudis of this world I can assure you, and you will have them thick and fast in the coming years.'

Lisa, delighted as she secretly felt at the alteration in her appearance, was in an agony of self-consciousness; she searched wildly in her mind for a new topic of conversation to deflect Magda's attention from herself. 'I thought,' she said diffidently, 'that you were Hungarian, but you speak about Hungarians as if you were not.' 'I!' exclaimed Magda. 'I am *Slovene*.' She enunciated this word with dramatic emphasis, opening her eyes very wide the while. 'But I suppose you do not know what is *Slovene*.' She began to comb her hair. 'Oh yes,' said Lisa, 'I *do*. Slovenia is part of Yugoslavia.' 'My God!' cried Magda, 'you are indeed a genius, to know this. I have not before met an Australian who has heard of the place.' 'Oh, but we did the Balkans at school,' said Lisa; 'in the causes of the First World War, you know, in Modern History. Lots of us know about Slovenia, lots. There was a question in the exam paper, I did it.' 'You amaze me utterly,' said Magda. 'I was right to give you my belt. So you know of Slovenia. Well, some time I may tell you more of it, but not now. We must have our walk, it is pretty around here, it will please you. We will just show ourselves to the Hungarians as we leave.'

The two women made their adieux and Lisa was gratified by Rudi's reiterated invitation to her: 'I will see you at the party which Magda and Stefan have so wisely decided to give in my honour,' said he; 'and we shall arrange our visit to the Art Gallery then, shall we not? I look forward to it. It is never too soon to begin to cultivate one's sense of humour: if I can introduce you to the Art Gallery of New South Wales as it properly deserves, I shall not have lived in vain.'

23

Patty had not taken note of Lisa's extraordinary conference with Magda, although this was the sort of incident which normally elicited a sarcasm, and Fay couldn't help noticing that generally speaking Patty wasn't quite her usual self this Saturday morning. She had nothing whatever to say about Frank or about what they might mean to do this weekend, and that was all right, because Fay had after all had no reciprocal information to divulge about her own weekend plans, and the two women went about their work in an atmosphere of abnormal self-containment, Patty never caring what Fay might be concealing, and Fay never wondering what might be occupying the silent thoughts of Patty.

The morning had been mercifully a little cooler; there was a fresh breeze, and even now as she left to go home Patty felt the sunshine to be more pleasant than oppressive. She jumped onto her tram with a light heart: not even a Saturday morning in Ladies' Cocktail had quite obliterated the strange sensations which had possessed her body and her mind since the events of the night before. But mingled with this pleasant and even mysterious feeling of disorientation, of translation into another element, was a shiver of fear and even of foreboding.

Frank had never before behaved quite as he had done last night; not even on their honeymoon had he so behaved; never before had Patty experienced the sensations she now so strangely experienced; never before had she sat on a bench in the tram feeling that she had just been allowed to learn a secret – but a secret so rare that there were no words for it, so rare that it was never mentioned or even alluded to, so rare that it might be the sole property of her and Frank. And the thought that it might be their sole property was one of its fearsome aspects, for they had never shared a secret before: this secret placed them in a different relationship with each other. Patty did not articulate all this to herself as fully as it has been articulated here, but it was nonetheless articulated at some level of apprehension effectively enough for her now to be able to feel, and with justification, that it would be fearful, as well as exciting, to see Frank again – Frank alert and conscious, Frank awakened once more from the deep sleep in which she had left him this morning to come in to work. What would he do, what would he say? This would be their first fresh encounter in this new secret-sharing world: Patty walked home from the tram stop in a dizzy state of mingled desire and apprehension, and as she opened her front door she felt her heart beating loudly.

The house was possessed by a silence which seemed in the circumstances awesome, and for a terrible moment Patty expected Frank suddenly to spring at her like a monster from behind a piece of furniture. But where, at this time of all times, was he? Could he really have gone out now, could he really at this time of all times have left her to return to an empty house, to his entire absence: have left her to experience by herself this strangeness, this solitary possession of their shared secret? It could hardly be possible. She glanced into the bedroom: it too was empty; the bed was unmade.

She went slowly, still astounded and marvelling, into the kitchen; then she proceeded by ever slower steps to make a complete tour of the house. It shunned her with its silence; she and it were quite alone. She returned to the kitchen and sat, dully wondering, as the sensation of strange pleasure drained away from her, leaving only the sensation of fear, and when by the dinner hour Frank had not appeared, the sensation of fear began to take on vivid and dreadful life, and to create vivid and dreadful shapes in her imagination. By the time she went to bed she felt stunned, except that, busily in her mind, these vivid and dreadful shapes sported and played.

24

The water in the Harbour had turned dark blue by the time Magda returned to the flat: the afternoon was dying, sweetly, gently, as it does at that latitude. Stefan offered to make some tea. 'Did you have a nice walk?' asked Rudi, who appeared to have settled in for the evening. 'Shall we go to a concert? There is a chamber music recital at the Con.' 'You and your culture,' said Magda. 'I feel like a film. Let us not decide now. I must telephone Lisa's mother to tell her that her daughter is safely en route, our walk took us further than was planned, she may be anxious.' She went into the bedroom to telephone and returned a few minutes later. 'How strange,' she said; 'she does not seem to know the name of her own child; "Lesley" she pronounces it. This Australian speech is very bizarre.' 'Yes, not the English I should care to hear my own children speak I must say,' said Rudi. 'Which is an imminent problem,' said Stefan to Magda. 'Rudi here has been telling me that he wishes to marry.' 'Of course you do,' said Magda, 'why not? But all in good time. At the moment you are still looking for a girlfriend, not to mention a flat.' 'To tell you the truth,' said Rudi, 'I am looking for a girlfriend suitable for elevation to the position of wife. I wish to marry soon. I am tired of the junket of girlfriends: I want to settle down.' 'I can't think of a single one of our friends who is the right age, or who has a daughter of the right age either,' said Magda. 'You may have to arrange this matter yourself, God knows how.' 'I am not fussy,' said Rudi. 'No, you will only want a beauty, less than thirty years old, cultivated, if not also rich; it should be quite easy,' said Stefan.

'Certainly I want a beauty,' said Rudi, 'the age is less important. Cultivated – well – I have heard that there is such a thing—' 'What do you take us for?' said Stefan. 'Naturally we are cultivated, we reffos, we are famous for it, or rather notorious, it is one of our most despicable qualities.' 'Oh, you have misunderstood me!' said Rudi. 'I am not looking for a reffo; I have decided to marry an Australian.' 'You must be mad!' cried Magda. 'What do you imagine she will want with you? An Australian. The cultivated ones are anyway all either married, or else they have gone away.' 'Gone away?' asked Rudi. 'Where have they gone?' 'They go away to London, sometimes Paris or even Rome,' said Stefan. 'You will hardly ever find one here; if you do she is saving her fare to London, I can guarantee it.' 'Well then,' said Rudi, 'I will take an uncultivated one and cultivate her myself. I should enjoy that.' 'Psssht,' said Magda. 'Leave the poor girl alone. She is happy as she is.' 'Do you really think so Magda?' asked Rudi. 'Be honest. Did you ever see such—' 'As a matter of fact, no,' said Magda. 'I am afraid you are quite right. Very well, you wish to meet an Australian, uncultivated, you will make her happy, or happier, perhaps cultivated too. It is all quite simple.'

'A nice, strong, healthy Australian girl. Some of them are very beautiful,' said Rudi. 'Haven't you noticed? That is what I would like.' Stefan laughed. 'Oddly enough,' he said, 'we know no one of this description, no one at all.' 'This is true,' agreed Magda. And then she was struck by a thought. 'As a matter of fact,' she said, 'this is *not* true. I do know such a one. She is about thirty or less, she is not quite beautiful, but not bad, her *maquillage* is terrible of course and she has no style, but she is strong and healthy as far as one can see, and now I think about it I must say she has by no means the air of a woman in love.' 'I am very desirous of meeting her,' said Rudi; 'do please arrange it.' 'I'll see,' said Magda. 'I do not know whether you deserve her. I'll see. Now, shall we go to see a film, or not? Let us decide.' And they began to argue the pros and cons of the available films, and the chamber music programme, as the darkness swiftly fell.

25

It was almost six o'clock when Lisa at last reached home. She burst through the back door, still glittering with the elation of the afternoon, to find her mother standing at the sink peeling potatoes. 'Hello Mum!' she cried. 'Look!' and she smiled like a film star and whirled around on the spot. Her mother regarded her with a face like a hot-cross bun.

'I should think I would just look!' she said. 'I should think I would. Now perhaps you'll tell me what on earth you've been up to. I've had a telephone call from that Magda you've been with, Mrs Zombie-something, who rang to say you were on your way home, and she doesn't even seem to know your name! Maybe it's her funny accent, but she tried to tell me – me! – your name is *Lisa*. Imagine! And here you are so late home, and where are your glasses? Did you leave them behind? And why are you so late? You told me you'd be home at four o'clock: I don't know what to think!'

Lisa's elation vanished in the moment and she sat down suddenly on a nearby chair. She took her glasses from her bag and put them on the kitchen table, and sat hunched over, thinking. Then she took the lipstick from her bag, and opened the case. It was an expensive kind, in a heavy gold metal container; the colour was called 'Angel's Kiss'. She painted her lips, and then she held out the lipstick. 'Magda gave me this,' she said. 'Would you like to try it? It tastes nice, too.' She pressed her lips together. 'She gave me this, too,' she added, pulling at her belt. 'Do you like it?'

Her mother stared at her, speechless. 'I'm sorry I was late, Mum,' Lisa continued, 'but we went for a walk, and it took longer than I thought it would. We looked at all the houses, and Magda talked about Slovenia. That's where she comes from. And then I had to walk up to Spit Road, and the tram didn't come for ages. I'm sorry, honestly.'

'I don't know what to think, Lesley,' said her mother. 'I've never seen you like this before. I don't know what to think.' 'There's nothing *to* think,' said Lisa. 'But Mum, I wish you'd call me Lisa, too. That's what they all call me at Goode's. I told them that was my name. It's on the form and everything.' 'It's what!' exclaimed Mrs Miles. 'It's what! What do you mean? Your name is Lesley!' 'But I don't like it,' said the girl. 'I want to be Lisa. And I will be. And I am!' And she burst into tears at the same moment as her horrified and overwrought mother began to weep. The two women cried separately for a minute, and then Lisa looked up. Mrs Miles was wiping her eyes on her apron. 'Lisa,' she said; 'Lisa. How do you think it feels to have your own child telling you she wants a different name? You've always been Lesley to me, you always will be. What's wrong with Lesley? It's a lovely name. Lisa. It's like a slap in the face. Perfect strangers—'

'Magda's not a perfect stranger, she's my friend,' said Lisa. 'Some friend!' cried Mrs Miles. 'I don't even know her!' 'Well, that's not my fault,' said Lisa. 'She's still my friend, and so is Stefan.' 'Who's Stefan?' asked Mrs Miles, alarmed. 'Only Magda's husband,' said Lisa. She thought she had better not mention Rudi just now. 'He's very nice. We talked about books. And I'm going to their New Year's Eve party too, *if you'll let me*. Magda said I had to ask your permission.' 'I should think so!' said Mrs Miles. She looked down at the linoleum; secretly she was somewhat mollified by this piece of Slovenian politesse. 'I'll see,' she said. 'But Lisa! Lisa! How could you do such a thing? To change your name like that, and not a word to me. It's so sly.'

'Oh Mum,' said Lisa. 'I didn't mean to be sly, I didn't. I just wanted – I wanted a real girl's name. Lesley is a *boy's* name.' 'It's a girl's name too,' said her mother. 'It's spelt differently for a boy.' 'But it sounds the same,' said Lisa; 'that's what counts. I wanted a proper girl's name, for when I grew up. I've been a child for so long now; I want to be grown up.' 'Oh Lesley –' said her mother; 'Lisa. If you only knew what being grown up can be like, you wouldn't want to do it any faster than you have to.' 'Oh Mum,' said Lisa, suddenly appalled: and she got up and went over to her mother and they put their arms around each other. Mrs Miles's eyes had filled again with tears which began to slide down her cheeks. 'Please don't cry, Mum,' said Lisa. 'Oh dear, I don't know what to think,' sobbed Mrs Miles. 'I suppose I always knew I'd lose you one day, I just didn't expect it to happen so soon!' And she wept more loudly.

'Mum, Mum, *please* don't cry,' said Lisa, on the verge herself of fresh tears. 'You haven't lost me, you aren't *losing* me: you'll never lose me. You're my mother, how could you lose me? I'll stay with you *always*.' 'Now Lesley, Lisa, you know you can't say that,' said her mother, wiping her eyes again. 'You'll marry, or you'll go away, even go abroad – all the girls do that now. You can't stay with me always, can you? It wouldn't be right. I'm just being selfish, I suppose.' 'No, you're not,' said Lisa. 'But even if I marry or go away, you'll still be my mother, and I'll always see you, often.' 'I hope so,' said Mrs Miles. They glimpsed the long prospect before them and turned their eyes away from its impossibly mysterious and even tragic vistas. 'Just try to be a good girl, Lesley,' said her mother. 'That's what matters.' 'Of *course* I will,' said Lisa. 'You can go on calling me Lesley if you like,' she added. Her mother now at last smiled. 'I'll see,' she said. 'I'll have to see what I think. I might manage to call you Lisa sometimes, if you're very good. It depends.' They both laughed and let go of each other. 'But right now I'd better get on with my potatoes,' said Mrs Miles, turning back to the sink. As she did so, she looked at Lisa from the corner of her eye. The girl was leaning over the kitchen table, retrieving her glasses and the lipstick and her handbag, and Mrs Miles was struck by the feminine grace of her form, set off by the wide leather belt. 'You know, that belt looks really nice,' she said. 'It must be a very good one. Magda was very kind to give it to you, it must have been very expensive. I hope you thanked her for it properly.' Lisa smiled brilliantly. 'Of *course* I did,' she said. '*And* for the lipstick. Do you want to try it now?' 'I will later,' said her mother. 'It's a very nice colour, it looks very nice on you. I must say you do look very nice: Magda must like you, to go to so much trouble.' 'Well, I suppose so,' said Lisa, uncertainly. 'But I can't think why,' said Mrs Miles. 'No, me neither,' said Lisa, 'a horrible girl like me.' 'Well, you're still growing up,' said her mother; 'you've got a bit of time. You might be quite nice in a few years: we'll have to see. Right now I want you to sit down and shell those peas for me.' 'So can I go to the party?' asked Lisa. 'I'll see,' said Mrs Miles. 'Just shell the peas first, and I'll think about it.' There was silence for a time, and then she was heard to say, half to herself, '*Lisa*. I never.

26

As soon as Fay got home from Goode's, she began to attack her flat. The area of battle was not large: it consisted of a medium-sized room with two armchairs and a divan bed and a few occasional tables, and a kitchenette. She shared a bathroom which she was not obliged to clean but often did. When she had dealt with her flat she did her laundry in her landlady's copper and hung it all out on the clothesline where it flapped wildly in the ocean breeze, and then she had a bath and washed her hair and did her nails.

She had finished *The* Women's *Weekly* by dinnertime, so when she had cooked herself some macaroni cheese she sat down on the floor to eat it, propping *Anna Karenina* open at the first page, and she began to read. Late on Sunday night she said to herself, it's really amazing how fast time goes by when you're reading a book. I never realised.

27

Mrs Crown was on the telephone, sitting by the little table where it was kept in her hallway. 'What do you mean, you're not coming over?' she was saying. 'I've got a big leg of lamb here specially, it's just gone in, and I've already done the vegetables. What do you mean, you're not coming?'

Patty shuddered with fright and confusion. This was proving to be more difficult even than she had imagined: it was a nightmare. 'But Frank's not feeling well,' she said. 'He's not up to it.' 'Frank not well!' exclaimed her mother, 'I never heard of such a thing. Frank's always the picture of health. What's the matter with him?' 'Oh, I don't know,' said Patty, 'it's nothing, he just needs a day to himself. He's lost his appetite, he feels crook.' 'Well, perhaps he needs a doctor. Have you had the doctor?' asked Mrs Crown. 'Oh no,' said Patty, 'I don't think he needs the doctor. I'll see how he is tomorrow.' And then she began to cry.

'Patty Williams, or Crown as was,' said her mother, 'I'm coming right over there, even if the lamb has gone in. I'll turn it off and come right over, even if it is ruined. If you won't tell me what's going on I'll just come and see for myself. I don't care about the lamb if you don't.' 'No!' sobbed Patty, 'leave the lamb in. I'll come over, I'll come myself. Just give me a bit of time to get ready.' She wasn't even dressed yet; she had awakened in the empty bed at six a.m. and had been sitting almost catatonic with fear and shock in her kitchen ever since, staring at the front page of the Sunday paper. 'I'll come over as soon as I can,' she said. 'Leave the lamb in.'

She looked through the coloured glass panels surrounding her mother's front door as she had done as a child, and rang the bell. 'Patty,' said Mrs Crown, standing on her doorstep in a pinny, 'now perhaps you'll come in and explain yourself.' They proceeded down the long narrow hallway to the kitchen where the lamb could be heard loudly sizzling in the oven. The table was already set for five. 'Oh God,' said Patty, sitting down suddenly in a heap, 'is Joy coming?' 'No, just Dawn and Bill,' said Mrs Crown. 'The kids are all at the beach with the neighbours.' 'That's something,' said Patty; 'I couldn't face Joy.' Mrs Crown put the kettle on. 'I'm going to make some tea,' she said, 'and you're going to tell me what's going on. Now.'

'Frank's disappeared,' said Patty. 'He what?' asked her mother. 'He's gone,' said Patty. 'He was gone when I got home yesterday. He hasn't come back.' 'Have you told the police?' asked Mrs Crown, pale with shock. 'He might've had an accident.' 'They said not to worry yet,' said Patty. 'They said people do it all the time. They said to come to the station and fill in a Missing Persons form if he doesn't turn up after a week. A week!' And she burst into tears.

Her mother sat beside her and patted her shoulder. 'There,' she said, 'there now. You cry for a bit.' Patty cried for some time. 'I don't understand it, Patty,' said Mrs Crown. 'Have you had a row?'

'No!' cried Patty. She could hardly tell her mother what they had done instead. A row! The memory of the strange shared secret was now like a dream, something which had not actually happened. 'I don't understand it either,' she said. 'I really don't.' And she began again to cry. 'Listen, Patty,' said Mrs Crown. 'I'll tell you this. No one understands men. We don't understand them, and they don't understand themselves. That's flat. That's why they do these wicked stupid things, like going off. I could tell you some stories! But they always come back, in the end. Usually, anyway. The ones that don't, aren't worth it, believe you me. He'll come back. You'll see. They can't really manage by themselves, men can't. They think they can, but they can't. They're just children.'

At this word Patty's tears increased, and her mother continued to pat her shoulder. 'Now then, Patty,' she said, 'you dry your eyes. Go and wash your face and we'll have some tea. I'm going to put the vegetables in.' She got up, and Patty went to the bathroom. When they were drinking the nice hot tea Mrs Crown looked at her daughter. Poor little Patty, the one in the middle: she had always been squashed by the determined Dawn, the assertive Joy: she was a bit of a mystery even to her own family, was Patty. 'You know I like your hair a bit longer,' said Mrs Crown. 'Why don't you grow it out for a bit? It suits you.' 'Yes,' said Patty dully, 'I might.' 'Meanwhile,' said Mrs Crown, 'what did Frank take with him? Did he take many clothes?' 'I never thought to look,' said Patty. 'I just waited, I thought he'd come back any minute.' 'So he might,' said her mother, 'but it won't do no harm to look. I'm coming back with you later and we'll have a good look. Then you can get some things and come and stay here with me, while he's gallivanting around, the selfish bugger, causing grief.' 'No!' cried Patty, 'I have to stay at home, in case he comes back!' 'Humph!' said Mrs Crown. 'He doesn't deserve it. You think about it. Serve him right if he came back and found you gone. Selfish, they all are. They never think.'

'Please don't tell Joy,' said Patty. 'Or Dawn.' 'Well, I don't know,' said Mrs Crown. 'We can't say he's ill, can we? Dawn won't believe that any more than I did. I know. We'll say he's gone away for a few days on business – that's all right, isn't it? He used to do that when he was a travelling salesman there. We can say he's filling in for someone else for a few days. Then we'll see what happens. It's too bad just before Christmas and everything. He'd better come back by Christmas, that's all I can say, or he'll have some explaining to do to me, that's all I can say!' And Mrs Crown looked properly fierce, and Patty, almost to her surprise, felt strangely comforted, and began even to feel quite fierce herself. He was a selfish bugger. They all were. But they couldn't manage by themselves.

28

The scene which met the military eye of the Ruritanian army officer, as he ushered Lady Pyrke through the doorway of Goode's at eleven a.m. on Christmas Eve, was pandemonium, with sound effects complete. To the obligato of a hundred intense conversations between the black-clad staff and their customers were added the shrill ringing of cash register bells, the cries of lift attendants – Going Up! – and the unhappy shrieks of children large and small whom it had been impossible to park with neighbours: the women of Sydney, or a frightening proportion thereof, were still doing their Christmas shopping, and it could only, so the lieutenant-colonel observed to himself, get much worse as the day wore on, for after lunch the office workers let off early, as so many of them were on this day, would swell the throng. Lady Pyrke sailed sedately down the marble stairs into the mêlée as if stepping into the waters at Baden Baden: at a time like this, thought the lieutenant-colonel, it really pays to be non compos mentis: good luck to the old girl. He watched her proceeding serenely to the handkerchief counter and turned back to face the street.

The scene on the second floor was a little quieter. Here an atmosphere merely of contained frenzy had been achieved: it was astonishing, thought Mr Ryder, how many ladies seemed to leave it to the last minute to buy their Christmas frocks, but here they all were, going into the fitting rooms with several over their arms to try on at once, and much consequent confusion for his staff who were already hard pressed. There was Lisa now, emerging from the fitting rooms half-smothered in assorted cocktail frocks retrieved after customers had found, or not, the one which suited them: if nothing else in their brief lives had rendered these frocks fit to be marked down, he observed, this last Christmas shopping day must: they would hereafter be good for nothing but the sales.

Even Model Gowns seemed to be doing business which verged on the vulgarity of being brisk. Mr Ryder noted with satisfaction that Magda – the inimitable! worth every penny! – was at the moment attending – but with such calm, such inflexible tact – to no less than three different customers: and *that* was at least five hundred guineas' worth of business on the hoof: if that wasn't a lovely sight, he would eat his hat.

There was Fay Baines, taking a handful of notes from a satisfied customer, with four more waiting their turn, and Lisa again with a great armful of frocks returning to the rails; Miss Jacobs stolidly explaining matters to an *echt* North Shore matron wanting a size they hadn't got in a model they had, and Patty Williams looking awfully pale and even – well, on the verge of – interesting, as she wrote out a charge form: if you want to get sick, Mrs Williams, he thought, just wait until five-thirty p.m., there's a dear. He smiled encouragement at them all as he proceeded on his rounds.

At lunchtime Lisa after changing ran out into the hot and

thronging city to buy her Christmas presents. She had done the necessary research during the previous week and now she dashed along to Grahame's and purchased a copy of *The* Story *of British Bloodstock*, extensively illustrated and bearing on its dustjacket the fine portrait of the Godolphin Arab, for her papa; in Rowe Street she bought a tiny snuff box made from a seashell for her mother. The total expenditure came to slightly more than one week's wages. In the canteen afterwards she saw Patty Williams looking rather ill. I wonder if I should speak to her, she thought. But she didn't: there was a forbidding expression on Patty's face which she had never seen before: neither had anyone else.

Oh the bastard, Patty was thinking, the bastard. The selfish, selfish bugger, leaving me to cope like this; who does he think I am? It was the ancient question and it had now occurred at last to Patty. Just run off, without a word, and left me to cope: thanks. It had been only this morning when she awoke that Patty had suddenly realised that if Frank had absented himself from home he was likely to have done so no less from work, and that she had better try to make his excuses in that quarter. But what – dreadful thought – if he were absent only from home? During her lunch hour she telephoned her mother to ask her to ring Frank at work in order to discover whether or not he were there; then having waited for ten minutes she telephoned her mother once more. 'He's not there,' Mrs Crown informed her, 'I didn't tell them anything. I didn't tell them who I was or anything. They just said Mr Williams hasn't come in today, they suppose he's crook but he hasn't let them know yet. They said to ring you if I wanted to know any more. Humph! You'd better phone them now, tell them he's sick and you don't know when he'll be back, that'll do for the moment.'

Once she was actually speaking to Frank's boss – *the slimy bastard* – who sounded perfectly nice to Patty, a perfect gentleman –

Patty discovered how easy it is once the lie is begun to make it sound exactly like the truth. She surprised herself. 'He's not well,' she said. 'I don't think he'll be back this week at all, really. I'd say he'll be away until the New Year; I'm real sorry.' 'Gee, Mrs Williams, that's terrible,' said Frank's boss. 'You tell him to put his feet up and not come back till he's quite fit, we'll manage; this is a slow week here anyway. We'll hope to see him straight after the New Year holiday; you let us know if he needs longer. I hope you have a happy Christmas anyway. Bye-bye for now.' Thank God that was done. But the bastard: the selfish bastard. Leaving her to cope. Where was he: what was he doing? He had taken the old travelling bag and a few clothes, and all of his fortnight's wages less the housekeeping which he had already given her on the Thursday night. He'd meant to go: he'd known what he was doing. There was no excuse. Selfish, completely selfish. *Who did he think she was?*

29

The frenzy mounted steadily throughout the afternoon, taking on an edge of hysteria at around four o'clock and liquefying into near panic at five. The last thirty minutes made demands on the staff of F. G. Goode's which their native stoicism alone enabled them to meet; but at last the ultimate Christmas sale was made, the crowd was all expelled, and the great glass and mahogany doors were closed and bolted fast.

Fay dashed up the firestairs to change and retrieve her travelling bag: if she were to get to Central Station in time to meet Myra for the early evening train to the Blue Mountains she had not a minute to spare. Patty followed her slowly: the dreadful day was ended, the more dreadful evening now threatened: appalling as was Frank's mysterious absence, the thought of his possible return, of meeting him once again in these new and awful circumstances, was in a way more appalling still. She moved wearily towards her locker: it was strange how very tired she felt: it was not the exhaustion of the day's work, but a lethargy more deadly, almost like sickness, and the journey home seemed an immense undertaking.

Lisa skipped up the stairs with a light heart: there was Magda, to whom she had had no chance to speak throughout the extraordinary day. She called her friend, who turned. 'Ah Lisa,' she said with her best smile, 'how are you this evening? Stimulating, this Christmas Eve nonsense, is it not? I have sold *four* Model Gowns this afternoon all to ladies who are attending the party tonight of Mrs Martin Wallruss, they feared at the last minute to be outdone. I am laughing like a drain. Tell me, did you ask your mother if you may come to my party? There is no need to acquire the couture model in order to attend in style, anything you happen to have will do very well.' 'Oh yes, I did,' said Lisa. 'She asked me to thank you, she says I can come – I *am* looking forward to it!' 'Very good,' said Magda. 'And let me wish you and your family a happy Christmas now – here!' And she kissed Lisa on each cheek. 'Now,' she said, 'there is someone else to whom I must say a word pronto – goodbye, Lisa.'

Fay was just emerging from the locker room when Magda laid an elegant hand on her arm. 'If I may detain you for just five seconds,' said she, with a charming smile. 'Me?' asked the astonished young woman artlessly. Magda laughed. 'I have to make a request of you,' she explained. 'My husband and I are having a New Year's Eve party – we would be so glad if you could come. There will be many people, some at least I hope will interest you – you would be doing us so great a favour, for the fact is we are slightly short of young ladies – is it not ridiculous? It is usually young men who are so thin on the ground. What is a party without many attractive girls? Please say you will come – Lisa will be there so you will not feel a complete stranger.' 'Well,' said Fay, quite unable to think – in a dreadful hurry, and in any case astounded by the invitation – 'thank you, I suppose I could come – New Year's Eve –

that would be real nice – yes, thank you!' *Merde*, thought Magda. Thank God that is done. Now Rudi has his healthy Australian girl, much good may it do him.

'You know that Magda,' said Fay to Myra as they sat on the train while it trundled through the suburbs on its way to the Blue Mountains, 'you know, who does the Model Gowns –' 'Oh yeah,' said Myra, 'I know.' 'Well, she's asked me to her New Year's Eve party.' 'Crikey! Are you going?' Myra had tried to persuade Fay to come in a large party of acquaintances to the New Year's Eve gala night at her club, when she herself would be very much on duty, in a new emerald green chiffon number with an orchid worked in silver and black sequins on one shoulder. 'Well, I said I would,' said Fay. 'You never know.' 'It might be good,' said Myra. 'Those Continentals always have nice food and drink, anyway. They know that much. You might even meet someone interesting, who knows?' 'Oh, I think they'll all be Continentals,' said Fay. Then she suddenly thought: like Count Vronsky. He must've been a Continental. 'Do Russians count as Continentals?' she asked Myra. 'Who are you thinking of?' asked Myra. 'Oh, no one in particular,' said Fay. 'I just wondered.' 'Well, I suppose they do,' said Myra. 'But you know they're not allowed out, Russians. You never really see any Russians, do you? They're all in Russia.' 'I suppose you're right,' said Fay. 'Still, if they *were* allowed out, they'd be Continentals, don't you think?' 'Oh yes, I reckon so,' said Myra. 'All them people are Continentals.'

30.

Dawn was on the telephone talking to Joy. 'Don't you say *anythink*,' she said severely. 'Don't you let on one word or I'll never speak to you again. It's Christmas after all.' 'I don't see what difference that makes,' said Joy. 'He's gone, hasn't he? Christmas or no Christmas. We have to know sooner or later, it might as well be sooner.' 'Now you just listen to me, Joy,' said Dawn sternly. 'I promised Mum *faithfully* not to let on I knew a thing. She made me swear. I've only told you because I reckoned you'd guess something was up anyway and cause more trouble trying to find out. So you're not supposed to know a thing.' 'Oh yes, typical,' said Joy, 'typical. I'm the youngest so I'm not meant to know anything that's going on even in me own family. Typical. Well, I can always find out, I don't need your help, do I?'

'Honestly, Joy,' said her exasperated elder, 'have a heart. I've *told* you what's going on, I've told you as much as I know. I just don't reckon it's a good idea to go blabbing about it on Christmas Day. And how would you like it? She's trying to put a good face on, she doesn't want to talk about it, it stands to reason. So just keep quiet, okay?' 'Oh, if you say so,' said Joy airily, admiring her smart new sandals which she had just bought at Farmer's, bugger the Goode's staff discount. 'I don't care, I just think it's ridiculous to have to pretend, with your own family. I wouldn't want to pretend, if it was me it happened to.' 'No, well you're different, aren't you?' said Dawn. 'Everyone isn't like you. Patty likes her privacy, doesn't she?' 'Patty likes her secrets, you mean,' said Joy. 'She always was that secretive. Well, she can keep her secret for all I care.'

'Good,' said Dawn. 'So you won't say anythink. And don't say anythink to Mum either because she doesn't know I've told you. She only told me because she was that worried. She said do you think he's gone for good? and I said of course not Mum. Frank won't get far. I had to say that to stop her worrying about Patty. But I don't know. Frank's a dark horse, I've always thought so.' 'Oh God,' said Joy, 'Frank's not a *dark horse*, Frank's a drongo. Get far! He couldn't get from here to Manly without a guide. He's just buggered off somewhere in a stew, he'll be back, worse luck. Poor old Patty.' 'That's no way to talk now,' said Dawn. 'Frank's all right, he's just a bit—' 'Stupid,' said Joy. 'Dim.' 'Quiet, I was going to say,' said Dawn. 'And he's being even quieter at the moment,' said Joy, cackling with laughter. 'Joy,' said Dawn, 'you're awful.' That was Joy all over: awful.

'Anyway at least we know one thing,' said Joy cheerfully. 'What?' asked her sister. 'We know it's not another woman,' said Joy. 'What do you mean, another woman?' said Dawn. 'What do you think I mean? I mean, it's *obvious* Frank hasn't left Patty for another woman.' 'How do you know that?' asked Dawn, unsure on whose behalf she ought to take offence at Joy's assertion. 'For God's sake, Dawn,' said Joy scornfully, 'just take a look, if you ever get another chance. Frank's not exactly Casanova.' 'Well, and a good thing too,' said Dawn stoutly. 'There's no need to go completely in the other direction,' said Joy. 'Frank doesn't hardly seem to know what women are for.' 'And what are women for?' asked Dawn. 'I'll draw you a picture,' said Joy, 'the next time I see you. And you can give it to Frank if he comes back. Then you'll both know.' 'Joy,' said Dawn, 'you're awful. And how come you know so much about Frank?' 'I can just tell,' said Joy, 'and anyway you only have to look at Patty. Etcetera. I think she's better off without him. She should buy some new clothes, have a good holiday, go to the Barrier Reef or somewhere, and start again.' 'Yes, well, that's one way of looking at it,' said Dawn, 'but I can't see Patty doing that.' 'No,' said Joy, 'that's too true. Never mind. I won't say anything tomorrow: we'll all have a real happy Christmas. Now what –' and the two sisters turned to one last conference on who was responsible for which viands on the morrow, when all her offspring and their husbands (where available) and their children (where present) were to converge on Mrs Crown bearing jointly and severally all the provender essential to a proper Anglo-Saxon Christmas dinner, with all the trimmings.

31

It was after six o'clock by the time Mr Ryder and Miss Cartright left Goode's on Christmas Eve; they were among the last few to leave the great edifice and a lackey waited by the Staff Entrance with a bunch of enormous keys, ready to lock the door.

A Jowett Javelin was double-parked by the kerb and Miss Cartright turned to her colleague. 'There's my young man,' she said. 'Can we offer you a lift? We're headed for Turramurra.' 'Now that is very good of you,' said Mr Ryder, 'but I'm meeting some friends at Pfahlert's for our annual get-together. Old school mates.' 'Enjoy yourself then,' said Miss Cartright, 'and have a very happy Christmas.' 'And you too Miss Cartright,' said Mr Ryder, raising his hat as she stepped into the impatient automobile.

He walked along Castlereagh Street through the now-diminishing throng and turned into the vastness of Martin Place. He had a fancy (who does not?) to walk along the GPO colonnade, and a moment after he had ascended the steps and begun his progress he realised that the figure at the nether end putting a letter through one of the fine brass-clad posting slots was their own Miss Jacobs. Strange time to post a letter, he thought. She's missed the Christmas post by several lengths. And there was something so sad about the picture she made – that lone, dumpy, self-contained figure, with her hair in a bun, with her half-empty string bag, posting her mysterious letter – that he almost wanted to run down the colonnade and catch her up, and then – well, it was futile. He could hardly hope to gladden what appeared to be such a lonely and indeed secret existence – he could hardly, for instance, offer her a drink. An ice-cream, perhaps. 'Would you care to accompany me to Cahill's, Miss Jacobs? We might have a Chocolate Snowball together.' Then he remembered Pfahlert's. Well, not tonight, he thought. But perhaps one day. Oh Miss Jacobs. You poor, poor dear. Have a very happy Christmas.

32

'Now Lesley,' said Mrs Miles, 'I want you to eat a proper breakfast, you don't know how long it will be before you get your Christmas dinner, you know what your Auntie Mavis is like.' They were all to go this year for Christmas dinner to Mrs Miles's sister and her family who lived at Seaforth; Mrs Miles's large family took it in turns, more or less, to preside at the feast. 'No, I don't, we haven't had Christmas there before,' said Lisa. 'Of course we have, don't you remember? Four or five years ago, of course you remember. We didn't eat until well past three. So you want a proper breakfast. Do you want boiled or fried or scrambled?' 'Ugh,' said Lisa. 'Magda says you shouldn't eat eggs for breakfast, it—' 'I don't care what Magda says,' said Mrs Miles. 'Magda doesn't know everything. If you won't eat your eggs for breakfast you won't ever get fatter. You'll waste away. You're still growing. Just have some scrambled eggs now, I'll put some bacon in with them the way you like.' 'Oh, *okay*,' Lisa drawled, 'anything for a quiet life.' 'That's better,' said her mother. Mr Miles came in. 'Three eggs,' he said, fried, runny yolks, and four rashers of bacon. Is the tea made yet? I'll have some toast too while I'm waiting. I could eat a horse. I've seen horses that are fit for nothing else too come to think of it.' 'Can we open our presents now?' asked Lisa. 'What presents?' asked her father. 'Dad,' said Lisa, 'do you know what day this is?' 'Oh,' said Mr Miles, 'I suppose you mean Christmas presents. Well, I don't know about that. That's your mother's department.' 'We'll open our presents after breakfast,' said Mrs Miles. 'First things first.' The meal was at last concluded and they went solemnly into the sitting room where the presents were ranged at the foot of the Christmas tree. Lisa presented her gifts to her mother and father, the small and the larger, and her mother gave her father one large package and then gave her one small and two larger packages. An episode of unwrapping followed by exclamations of surprise and gratitude followed, at the end of which time it was suddenly apparent that Mr Miles had made no contribution to the exchange. 'Now then,' he said, 'I suppose you'll both be wanting something from me. I suppose that's fair enough. It's Christmas after all. Let me see what I can find.' He fished in his pocket and found some coins. 'That won't do,' he said. He fished in another pocket. 'That's more like it,' he said. 'Here now Lesley, you take that', and he handed her a ten-pound note. 'And this is for you, Cora,' he said. 'Happy Christmas both.' Mrs Miles looked down, bemused. He had given her a twenty-pound note. The sight of it alone was a novelty. 'Gee. Thank you, Ed,' she said. 'That's lovely.' Lisa had been squealing with delight the while. 'Gosh Dad,' she said. 'Thanks!' 'All right then,' said the paterfamilias, 'let's get going. Seaforth, eh? We might have a swim first. What do you reckon? We'll catch the Christmas tide!'

33

'Doreen's bringing a big ham,' said Mrs Parker to Myra, 'and the pudding, and John and Betty are bringing the chooks, so they can go in as soon as they get here. I'll just turn on the oven and have it ready. So if we can finish doing these veges before they all arrive there won't be anything more to worry about. Until the gravy.'

Myra was peeling five pounds of potatoes. There would be thirteen of them to dinner counting the toddler. Unlucky number, she thought. Better not count the toddler. 'Did you and Fay finish setting the table?' asked her mother. They were going to squash around the ping-pong table on the back verandah to eat this feast; it was now covered with Mrs Parker's best tablecloth, which she still had from when she was first married, but as it wasn't quite large enough there was a double-bed sheet underneath it. 'Sure,' said Myra. 'Fay's just folding the serviettes now, in shapes.' Fay had acquired this art in one of her cocktail waitressing years; she was making mitres. Mrs Parker put down her peeling knife and went to make sure for herself that everything was as it should be. 'Now that's just lovely,' she said to Fay. 'It looks real posh.'

Later on that day, many hours later, Fay was playing skipping games on the lawn with Myra's nieces while her nephews did rough things in trees and the toddler slept exhausted on a rug. The men were drinking beer and Myra and her mother and sister and sister-in-law gossiped together in deck-chairs. 'You want to find a husband for that Fay,' said Mrs Parker to Myra. 'None of your night-club riff-raff. Someone nice and steady. Look how she's playing with the girls. You can see she gets on with children. She wants to be married and have some of her own.' 'Well, I've done my best,' said Myra. 'But she's a bit particular.' 'So she should be,' said Mrs Parker. 'The sorts of men you see these days.' 'Now, Mum, what do you know about that?' asked Doreen. 'You'd be surprised,' said Mrs Parker. 'She means the sorts I go out with,' said Myra. 'Oh Lord,' said Doreen. She and Myra both laughed. 'Do you still see Jacko Price?' 'Oh, once in a while,' said Myra. 'I never want to hear that man mentioned again here,' said Mrs Parker looking stern. 'After what he did.' 'Oh, he's all right, Mum,' said Myra. 'There's lots worse.' 'Don't tell me,' said Mrs Parker. 'But I wish you could find someone nice, for Fay. She's a lovely girl. It's a shame she hasn't met anyone nice that she could marry. Poor thing, no family to speak of, she needs a husband.' 'Yes,' said Myra. 'I guess you're right.' 'Of course I am,' said her mother.

74

'Bad luck Frank having to be away,' said Dawn's husband Bill kindly. Patty looked wan. 'Yes,' she said. 'It can't be helped.' I wonder if they really know, she thought. I wonder what Mum's really told them.

They were all out in the back yard where they had dragged two tables which put together (there was a drop of two inches half-way along the total length) made a board sufficiently large to accommodate them all. There would have been room for Frank too. Patty wasn't feeling frightfully well: she had eaten very little and she was further discommoded by the sharp-eyed glances she had been getting at regular intervals from Joy. She was doing her best, she was doing her bloody best, she just wanted to be left alone. She had to think. They had just finished the pudding and were about to pull the crackers: Dawn was bringing out a great pot of tea and Joy followed with the cups. They're good girls, my girls are, thought Mrs Crown. I can't complain. Oh dear, poor Patty. Dear me. 'Pull this cracker with me, Patty,' she said. The bang was a terrible further strain on Patty's nerves. She found herself with a tiny slip of paper in her hand on which something was printed. 'What does it say?' asked her mother. Patty read it out. 'Laugh and the world laughs with you,' she read. 'Weep and you weep alone.' Then she burst into tears and ran into the house. 'Auntie Patty's not feeling well,' said Dawn to the children, 'so you try and behave yourselves. When you've finished pulling your crackers you can get down and go and play. Yes, you can make a cubby house in the rabbit hutch. Or you can play Lotto with your new set.'

Having distracted the children she gave Joy a dark and pregnant look and followed her mother into the house. Joy, alone with her husband and brother-in-law lit a cigarette. 'Well,' she said, 'I told Dawn it's ridiculous all this pretending. I knew it wouldn't work. That Frank is a selfish bastard though. Poor old Patty. I'd divorce him if I was her.' Bill looked uncomfortable; he wasn't sure where his primary loyalties must lie. Joy's husband Dave, who was doing very well and would do even better, offered his brother-in-law a cigar. 'He'll come back,' he said. 'It'll blow over. He just has to sort himself out. Poor blighter. Did you put that beer in the fridge like I asked you to, Joy? Then let's crack a few, I've got a real thirst after all that food.' Joy went off to help with the washing up, and found Patty at the sink. 'Never mind, Patty,' she said. 'He'll be back soon. You'll never know he's been gone.' Oh, that was the truth all right: that was the whole trouble. 'I don't know,' said Patty. 'I'll see. I'll see when he comes back.'

35.

First they had pâté de foie gras on very thin slices of toast, then they had duckling with black cherries, then they had a sort of *bombe surprise* with lots of glace fruit in it, and there was absolutely nothing to drink except champagne. They'd all done quite well this year and they expected they'd do quite well next year too. 'Things are not all for the best,' said Stefan, 'in the best of all possible worlds, as we know, but I think on the whole that a modicum of happiness is occasionally possible for the luckiest of us.' 'Stefan is becoming philosophical,' said Rudi, 'give the poor blighter another glass of fizz.' 'Not so much philosophical,' said Gyorgy, 'as sententious. Give him a punch, not too hard, but palpable.'

'Leave him alone,' said Eva. 'I do not allow my guests to punch each other on Christmas Day. To be philosophical or even sententious is his privilege on such an occasion. Let us drink a toast to the Commonwealth of Australia. What a country! I still cannot believe my fate. To finish up a subject of the English monarch – I ask you! Fill the glasses, Sandor. To the Commonwealth of Australia! And to the Queen!' Twenty glasses were raised to the accompaniment of much laughter and the toasts were drunk, and then the adult portion of the twenty assorted, chiefly Hungarian, Continentals present lit cigarettes and cigars. They sat for a long time talking and then they walked down the hill to Balmoral Beach and played a game which bore some faint resemblance to soccer. 'It is very beautiful here,' said Magda to Stefan as the sun went down, 'it really is.' 'Are you happy?' he asked her. 'Of course not!' said Magda. 'What a very vulgar suggestion. Are you?' 'Oh dear, I hope not,' said Stefan.

36

'Now, dear Lisa, if you will make sure that all the gowns are still in order as they are in my stock-book,' said Magda, 'it will be truly kind. Miss Cartright comes to me in half an hour or so and we will decide on the sale prices. Then this afternoon or tomorrow you will finish writing out the tickets for them and everything will be ready. Good. I hear that Mrs Bruce Pogue is to give a *grande fête* on New Year's Eve – poor thing, she does not realise it will clash with mine, I have skimmed already the cream – it will surprise me to death if a number of ladies do not come in here today or tomorrow looking desperate to obtain a frock for the occasion. They will ask me if they can have them at the sale prices, and I will tell them Ah no madame I regret that is not possible, I am so sorry. They will pay up, not to look cheap. *Vraiment on s'amuse ici.* Now here is the stock-book, take it and do what you can *ma chérie.*'

Lisa re-entered the scented fairyland of the Model Gown, noticing that a number of its denizens had been spirited away to the outside world since her last reconnaissance. Tara had gone, so had Minuit. Feeling almost ill with dread, she let her eye run down the list to discover as quickly as she could the fate of Lisette and, hardly daring, bade her eye then travel to the last column. The space was blank: the frock was still unsold: still here, on its hanger, waiting. Of course it was not, it could not be, waiting for her, but it remained in some frail sense hers for so long as it lived here in its mahogany cabinet at Goode's. She must now make quite sure that it really was here still.

She searched along the rail and found it easily – its white flounces stuck out gaily beyond the more sober margins of its neighbours, and she gently made a space in front of it the better to gaze upon it. Its loveliness increased with each viewing: it was, after all, a work of art. She stood still, absorbed in its contemplation.

Suddenly she became aware of a presence behind her and turning quickly, almost guiltily, she beheld Magda, smiling broadly. 'Ah Lisa,' exclaimed she: 'I am afraid you have fallen in love – I should have foreseen the danger! Yes, it is a nice little frock, even adorable, truly – I do not know why we have not sold it. Of course it is very tiny, much too small for most of our customers as well as being of course much too young for them although they do not care about that – Mrs Martin Wallruss has wanted it, can you imagine! – but I have saved it from such a fate more than once. *Eh bien*, it will have to go on sale, perhaps some girl with a lot of sense who has saved her dress allowance will come and rescue it. How is it? Let me see, a hundred and fifty guineas – not so expensive, I suppose it will go on sale at seventy-five, these white dresses get so grubby, it will have to be half price. But don't let me keep you, continue your chore.' And she sailed away, to all appearances unaware of the havoc her words had wreaked.

Seventy-five guineas! Lisa had not until then realised that in some corner of her mind she had begun to dream of possessing the frock, had even speculated that its sale price might just equate with her total earnings at Goode's, all, excepting what she had spent on Christmas presents, saved up in her Post Office money box. Now she watched Lisette vanishing into the wardrobe of a girl with a sensibly disposed dress allowance: now she fairly lost it; now she saw wrenched from her so-tentative hand her heart's desire; it was a moment of absolute desolation. Her spirits suddenly leaden, she continued with her task.

Ladies' Cocktail too was busy with preparations for the sales during this interregnum between Christmas and New Year and Lisa was occupied with much checking and sorting. The last-minute arrangements would be accomplished after the store closed on New Year's Eve: some of the staff would stay behind for the purpose, and then the sales would begin as soon as the doors opened on the second of January, and if you thought Christmas was a bunfight, Miss Jacobs told her, you wait until you see the sales! At lunchtime Lisa was more than happy to make her escape from Goode's; she sat by the Archibald Fountain and stared at the passers-by, troubled by an inchoate feeling of discontent and uncertainty which was not, she truly believed, the result merely of renewed anxiety about her examination results and their consequences, coupled with the unattainableness of Lisette: the worst of it was, that she had forgotten her book; she had nothing to read.

37

'It's my husband,' said Patty, sitting nervously on the edge of her chair. 'Yes?' said the physician. He wasn't her usual doctor: the latter was on holiday and Patty was seeing his locum, a stranger: young, sharp, clever-looking; intimidating. 'You see,' said Patty, 'my husband – he—' 'You know, Mrs – er – Williams: please tell me about your husband by all means, but it would be much the best thing if he came himself, there's really nothing much I can do for him otherwise.' 'Yes, well,' said Patty desperately, 'that's the thing, you see, he can't come, because he isn't here. He's gone away.' 'I think you'd better explain,' said the physician. 'Well, he went away just a week ago. I don't know where he's gone. He didn't tell me. But I'm worried about his job. I told them he was sick this week but they'll expect him back next week so I don't know what to tell them. I don't know what to do.' She began to cry. The physician sat and watched her. 'It doesn't sound like a situation which can go on indefinitely,' he said. 'Has he ever done this sort of thing before?' 'Oh no,' sobbed Patty. 'I don't know what came over him.' 'Have you told the police?' asked the physician. 'Yes, they said lots of people do it. They said most of them come back. I filled in a form, just tonight. Just in case he has an accident or something. I don't know. But I have to tell them something at his work if he doesn't come back next week.'

'I do see the difficulty,' said the physician drily. 'But I can hardly give you a medical certificate for a patient I haven't so much as seen; I'm sure you realise that.' Then his humanity suddenly got the better of his principles and he almost smiled at the tearful creature confronting him. 'Tell you what!' he said. 'How about this? If he hasn't returned by the New Year, telephone his boss, say the doctor – don't use my name – thinks he's got shingles. That should do it. Have you heard of shingles? No? Well, shingles are the ticket. You see, no one knows where they come from or why, and no one can say how long they'll hang around. The only thing anyone knows about shingles is that they're *bloody* painful and a person who's got them certainly isn't fit for work. If, I mean when, your husband returns he'll have to come for a consultation to get a medical certificate for the leave he's had, that is if he wants one, and we'll have to work out something more or less truthful. But tell them the doctor thinks it's shingles for the time being. Can't tell how long it'll last. How's that?'

'Thank you, doctor,' said Patty woefully. 'I'll tell them. Shingles.' 'What about you now, Mrs Williams? You look a bit peaky; understandable in the circumstances, of course, must take care of ourselves. Family, relations to look after you? Need moral support at a time like this. Try not to take it too hard. He'll come back, why not. Men do these things, don't know why – bottled up, poor at expressing their feelings, stupid really. Eating normally, sleeping? That's right. Come and see me again if there's anything you think I can do. Take it easy. All right, Mrs Williams. Goodnight.'

*

Patty was still feeling that tired, she could have gone straight to bed although it was only eight-thirty when she got home from the surgery. She watched television for a while and then she gave up the struggle and climbed into bed. In the darkness she suddenly remembered a song she had heard long, long ago – had they sung it at school, or what?

Swing low, sweet chariot, comin' for to carry me home
Swing low, sweet chariot, comin' for to carry me home.

She cried for some time and then she fell asleep.

38

'What if we took the sleeves out,' said Lisa. 'Could we do that?' 'Well, we *could*,' said her mother. 'But then you'd have to have some facings. Well, I suppose I could just put some binding around. That might be all right, no one would notice.' Lisa sat down and unpicked the sleeves, and her mother found some bias binding and sewed it around the armholes. Lisa put the frock on again.

It was the frock her mother had made for her to wear to the end-of-term dance at school; it was white broderie anglaise, with a gathered skirt and – now no longer – puffed sleeves. Lisa looked at herself in the mirror. 'If we let it down,' she said, 'don't you think that would be better?' 'Oh, you want it long, do you?' asked her mother. 'No, just longer,' said Lisa. She took it off and looked at the hem. There was a good five inches; her mother had never forsaken the habit of making large hems in all her frocks, as for a child. Her mother unpicked the hem. 'I'm afraid there'll be a mark,' she said. 'I'd better wash it.' It was almost dry by the evening, and Lisa ironed it and tried it on again. 'Well, it certainly looks more grown up,' said her mother. 'It looks very nice.' 'I think it needs a belt,' said Lisa. 'I could buy one tomorrow in my lunch hour. I might get a silver one.' 'Oh, that would be lovely,' said her mother. 'You'll look really nice in that with a silver belt, and your white sandals with the heels.' 'Oh, yes, it'll do,' said Lisa. 'It's only a party, it's not a *grande fête*.' 'It'll be lovely,' said her mother. 'You're very lucky at your age to be going to a party with grown-ups. You mind you behave nicely. Magda's very kind to ask you.' 'And Stefan,' said Lisa. 'Yes, and Stefan too,' said her mother.

I wonder what it'll be like, thought Fay. I wonder what her flat is like. Is it posh? Magda had written the address for her on a slip of paper. Mosman: I don't know anyone else who lives in Mosman, though Fay. A lot of those Continentals live over there. The flat is probably all done in modern: Continentals often seem to go in for modern. What will I wear?

She took out all the possibles and looked at them, wondering which might make the best impression on a Continental, someone who liked modern things. Well, I'll wear the green and white striped, she thought. That's the newest. She was very apprehensive: I wonder why she asked *me*, she thought. Magda, whose husband was called Stefan, and all their Continental friends. Will anyone want to talk to me? They're probably all old, anyway. Well, at least it's something different: I can go home early if I don't enjoy it. If at first . . . anyway, I'll just set my hair and do my nails now, and then I'll be all ready for tomorrow night. It'll make a change, at any rate. Try again. Oh God.

79

'Lisa! – you know Rudi of course who is over by the window, he has not seen you yet – but stand back, let me admire you – ooh la la, how charming you look this evening, a woman comes into bloom at night! – and here is Stefan: what will you drink? Give her some of the punch, Stefan, I suppose she must try that at least once in her life. Be careful, Lisa, he has put an atom bomb in it, it is deadlier than it looks – *voilà*.

'Come and meet Sandor and Eva, and here is their son Miklos, all right, Michael he insists on being now, he is dinky-die as they say, a proper Australian, he even forgets how to speak Hungarian, he has just left school like you – and if you will excuse me for the moment I see some new arrivals I must greet ... George, Anna, Bela, Trudi! at last – come in, have a drink, have two drinks, you must catch up – oh, you have brought your fiddle I see, that is wonderful! – yes, we have made space to dance as you see in case anyone feels the temptation – Fay, come and meet Bela, he will play the fiddle for you if you smile at him nicely, can I get you another drink? Stefan, over here I beg you . . .

'Milos, have you met Trudi? Anna, this is Lisa, who works with me, she is my tower of strength but she is clever, she will go on soon to greater things – Sandor, help yourself to more punch – ah! there is the doorbell again, excuse me . . . Janos, you know everyone, I think – champagne! a magnum! I love you the best – shall we keep it for midnight? So have some punch, if you dare, if you do not there is white wine or red – here is Lisa whom you do not know, and Fay – excuse me, Anton and Marietta have just arrived, I think they have brought some others with them, I had better be a good hostess—

'Laszlo, at last! Yes, all in good time but I think you are too late for she is already dancing with Rudi as you see, and he is better looking than you, still, there's no accounting for tastes. Come and meet Lisa – no, you are too late there too, she is dancing with Miklos who calls himself Michael. Well, dance with Anna – she is only talking to Stefan, I cannot think why: off you go.

'Ouf! Stefan, how is the punch? Good. Is everyone here now, can I relax? We invited fifty, I am sure there are at least seventy-five here, I don't know whether there will be enough food. Yes, what the hell. Give me some more punch, I am the one who must catch up. Fay is still dancing with Rudi, Lisa is talking to Miklos or Michael, *ça c'est bon.* Everyone seems to be enjoying himself, I think I might be allowed to follow their example, don't you? Ah, Bela is taking out his fiddle – no, let this record finish and then he will play. Give him another drink, he plays much better when he's drunk.

'Fay, how well you dance – I have been admiring you, what a shame you have not a better partner, still, he has enthusiasm. In a while Bela will play and you can learn a few Hungarian dances, they are quite easy – there now! We all hold hands, and then . . .

'Oh my God, I thought I would die of laughter just now – Stefan, how is the punch? You have made some more? You had a spare atom bomb then, did you? You think of everything. Look at Anton, I think he is going to fall out of the window. Give me another drink.

'Lisa, don't forget to eat or you will get drunk and your mother will never forgive me. Have some of these canapés – that's right, Michael, take the whole plate, you can eat them together, they will be yours alone, you young people need your sustenance. Ah, the music starts again, we dance …

'Have another drink, Stefan has made some more punch … Trudi … Laszlo … white wine or red? … Oh, a waltz, now that is nice … eat something … boum!

'Lisa, George and Anna will take you home, it is easy, they live in Lindfield – Fay? – ah, well if you can trust him to get so far – you have not seen his car, it is a jalopy, don't say I didn't warn you. Happy New Year! Good night, good night – good morning, yes! Drive carefully! Happy New Year! My God! I thought they would never go – two a.m. is it? or three? I thought so. I love you too – Happy New Year!'

40

The great doors were opened and the phalanx of grim-faced viragos cantered through the breach and down the marble steps: it took a good five minutes for the whole formation to pass him as the Ruritanian lieutenant-colonel, standing well clear, reviewed it. Well done, ladies, he said to himself: off to as fine a flying start as I have seen these dozen years.

This he knew was merely the advance guard: supplementary troops would continue to arrive in large numbers for the next hour, in slightly lesser numbers up until lunchtime, and in still-considerable force throughout the afternoon. The elite regiment of the first day would be replaced by the only slightly less determined battalions of the second and subsequent days, but look at it as one would, the scene at Goode's for the next ten days would be, not to put too fine a point on it, a battlefield; honours would be won, and indeed merited; trophies would be displayed; lives might not be lost but wounds of one kind or another would most certainly be sustained: the sale was now in progress.

Each floor of the great building revealed substantially the same sight: of hundreds of women, all caution, all dignity abandoned, fighting for their rights to possession of frocks, skirts, jerseys, shoes, blouses and hats at greatly reduced prices. Who could blame them, who so much as criticise? They were driven not by any impulse so mere as greed or vanity, but by a biological law which impelled them to make themselves fine: and now they hoped to fulfil its diktat without at the same time making themselves broke. They were treading the ancient and ever-fine line; a few of them were bound, by reason either of superior taste or of extraordinary luck, or both, to succeed in the enterprise. It was with such hopes that they came in their hundreds from distant Kogarah, faraway Warrawee, impossible Longueville and Wollstonecraft too, and the lieutenant-colonel wished them godspeed.

The *echt* North Shore matron was here; and so was Joy; and so was Myra, with commissions from Doreen as well as a few requirements of her own. The mother of Frank's boss's notorious sons was here and so were the sons themselves, all headed straight for Children's Shoes; and Mrs Miles had been prevailed upon by Lisa to at least *look* at the Sportswear and Casuals with a view to spending her twenty pounds on some new clothes for herself which she could simply put on her back with no more ado, and above all no slavery over a hot and vexing sewing machine. 'It's practically as cheap in the end, Mum,' said Lisa; 'because there's my staff discount on top.' So they were to meet in the lunch hour and review the situation to date.

Eva, Trudi, Anna and Marietta got here well within the first two hours of opening, and Dawn arrived just before lunch. She entered in the wake of Lady Pyrke, who had annually for the past thirty years or more arrived at just this hour on just this day for the purpose of acquiring one dozen new sets of underwear, heavily discounted; this solemnity accomplished, she would walk, steadily oblivious of the heat and the crowds, all the way to the Queen's Club where she would have a little poached fish and a long sleep, a copy of *Time and Tide* open on her lap. Her chauffeur had instructions to call for her at three.

The only exception to the scene of lawful bedlam was, of course, Model Gowns; there the flag of decorum might never be lowered. Those who might not be intimidated by their first glance at the prices, would be by an indefinable something in the eye of Magda. She knew at the slightest glance who her potential customers were: she knew not only who would buy this year, but also who might, with the right encouragement, return again to buy next: and she knew who would never buy. Upon Joy she might faintly have smiled; upon Dawn, she would barely perceptibly have frowned. As it was, here, just before three o'clock, were Mrs Martin Wallruss and Mrs Bruce Pogue, who having lunched together at Romano's were moving in for the season's final kill: three frocks for the price of two, with parties in their dozens still to come. The last column in Magda's stock-book began to fill up nicely, and Lisa, glancing across from the midst of the mayhem at Ladies' Cocktail, wondered in anguish if she would ever see Lisette again.

41

‘Rudi! what are you doing here? Do you want to buy *a frock*?’

‘My dear Lisa – I had quite forgotten that this is your bailiwick too. Isn’t that a splendid word, bailiwick. No, to tell you the truth – as you are my friend I hope you can keep a secret – I wish to speak a few words to Fay. Is she here? Oh, how unfortunate. Well, I shall wait until she returns. Perhaps I shall buy a frock after all – they are all so cheap at the moment it is a pity not to. Which do you recommend? This, now – would it suit me?’

‘Rudi, you must go away, Miss Jacobs will have a fit if she catches me talking to you. Go away and come back in ten minutes or so.’

‘Oh well, if you do not want me, I will say hello to Magda, where is she? Oh, I see, thank you. She will not want me either but I shall ignore that. Goodbye for the present.’

‘Fay, Rudi is here looking for you. He’s with Magda.’ ‘Oh God – I’ll just go over there and see him – thanks.’ There was no mistaking the gleam of delight which had sprung into her eye. Gosh, thought Lisa. So.

'Fay, at last. As I could not telephone you I came all the way here in my lunch hour to see you and ask you if you will risk an outing with me on Friday night. Please say yes. We might go to a film and then have dinner, or whatever you would prefer. Say yes in principle, we can discuss the details over the telephone if you will ring me tonight, here is the number. Oh, I am glad. Tonight then, don't forget!'

'Lesley, all right, *Lisa*, there's someone called Michael Foldes rang you up here just half an hour ago, he says he'll ring you again this evening. Oh, I see. Hmm. Well if he wants to take you out he has to pick you up here so I can meet him, even if he is a friend of Magda's, I don't know who he is, anyway how can he respect you if he doesn't meet your parents first or me at least. Yes, well, he'll just have to wait until Saturday night, he can wait that long if he really likes you, and so can you. I hope he isn't too old for you. No, well that's all right then. Shore, did he? Well, that should be all right. He sounded very nice, very polite. He doesn't sound Continental at all. Yes, well I suppose he is really an Australian then, if he *grew up* here. There's the telephone now, you answer it, it might be him again.'

'Dave said I could spend fifty pounds, so I had a look at the cocktail frocks, you know we've got that reception coming up, but I couldn't see anything I liked; I'll see what they've got at Farmer's or I might wait until the sales begin at Double Bay, I think there's one at Jay's next week. I got some things for the kids, did you? Yes, it's worth it. Yes, I saw Patty just for a moment but she was that busy I didn't really have time. Do you? Yes, but she's always so pale, there isn't that much difference. Well, what do you expect?

He's been gone nearly two weeks, it doesn't look as if he's in a hurry to come back. *If* he's coming back. It wouldn't surprise me if he's just shot through. Good thing too. No, well, she might miss him *now*, but she'll get over it. It's not as if she's got kids to remind her. There's no one to worry about except herself. She's got time to start again if she'd just pull herself together and smarten herself up a bit.

'Well, she's not a child for God's sake, she's old enough to look after herself, she's older than me, I can't be running around after her. Why doesn't she go and stay with Mum? She can leave a note for him, it's more than he bothered to do for her. If Dave did that to me I'd divorce him on the spot. All right, look, I'll phone her tonight, I'll find out what she wants to do at the weekend; she can come to the beach with us if she wants to, but she probably won't. All right, I said I would, so I will, but I can't see why you're making such a fuss. She's old enough to look after herself. Yes, all right. Ta-ta.' Joy put the receiver down and examined her fingernails. That's what I should have looked at, she thought. I knew I'd forget something. You can get some real bargains in cosmetics at the Goode's sale. Oh well. Must get the kids bathed. 'Kids,' she called. 'Inside now – bath time!' Remind me to ring Patty after I've fed them, she told herself. Oh, *gawd*.

42

Lisa had a few minutes in hand at the end of her lunch hour so she popped in to Model Gowns to say hello to Magda. '*Mon Dieu*!' exclaimed the latter. 'It has been a madhouse here. Look!' and she waved a hand towards the Model Gowns in their mahogany cabinets. Their ranks were indeed seriously depleted; Mrs Bruce Pogue and Mrs Martin Wallruss had been succeeded by others of their ilk and the frocks which now remained had very ample room to breathe. Lisa looked, hardly daring, and saw her beloved in the first glance. Magda noted her involuntary tremor. 'Oh, go and look,' she said. 'See if there is anything left to tempt you.' Lisa forced herself to laugh. 'I've found the one I want already,' she said. Magda looked at her again. Ah, well, it was after all a case of true love: she resolved suddenly to indulge it. There was in any case the more serious matter of the cultivation of the taste: if that should involve a degree of heartbreak, so be it. 'Oh yes, the little *robe de jeune fille*. Though I'm afraid all the *jeunes filles* with cash in this city have more the idea of attempting to look like women of the world, it is only their mothers who want to look young, that frock is no use to anyone when it is too small for *les mamans* and too young for *les débutantes*. I am tired of it: why don't you come in here in your lunch hour tomorrow after you have changed, and try it on? It is your size I think precisely. You can have a *fantaisie* for a few moments, it is good for the soul. Wear your high heels, to get the right effect.' 'Oh,' said Lisa, shaken, 'could I really? That would be wonderful . . .' 'Oh, it's nothing,' said Magda, 'but I won't be held responsible if I hear later that you have robbed a bank in order to buy it. Of course I may sell it between now and tomorrow – we'll just have to see.' 'Oh, *please* don't say that,' said Lisa; '*please* don't sell it.' 'That is a promise I could never make,' said Magda, laughing heartily and with sincerity.

Lisette was, of course, everything which could have been hoped, have been dreamed; like all the great works of the French couture, it was designed to look beautiful not simply as a thing in itself, but as the clothing of a female form. It took on then the property of vitality and movement: that is, of rhythm: it became finally incarnate. Lisa stood, overwhelmed, staring into the great cheval glass. She could see at the same time the back view reflected in the glass at the other side of the salon. She swayed very slightly, to see the effect of the three tiers of the skirt floating on the air. The frock fitted her exactly: the bodice was just short of being tight. Her arms and legs, appearing beyond the flounces at the shoulders, the hem, seemed now to be not thin, but slender. The frock changed her absolutely; the revelation which had come upon her when she had first been shown the Model Gowns was now complete.

There was nothing which needed to be said, and Magda herself was for once silent, at least for one entire minute. She smiled.

'Ah me,' she sighed. 'Shall we deliver it, Mademoiselle, or will you take it with you?' Lisa laughed. 'I'll wear it,' she said. 'Could you wrap my other clothes? Make out my bill as usual.' At this moment Miss Cartright appeared, coming to relieve Magda for the latter's luncheon break.

'How now,' she said. 'Is Lisa modelling for you now, Magda? We never thought of that.' 'It is her lunch hour,' said Magda. 'At this moment she is merely a customer, she is trying on a frock which has tempted her but the sale is not so far made.' 'Yes, I see,' said Miss Cartright. 'How big is the sting? Seventy-five, is it? It's a bargain all right.' 'You know,' said Magda, 'I'm wondering if it won't have to be a greater one still if it hasn't sold by the middle of next week. You see, it is getting dirty, they all do, these whites.' 'That's so,' said Miss Cartright. 'Well, fifty after next Wednesday, say, if it hasn't gone by then. But that isn't likely. How are we doing otherwise? Oh yes, I see. Jolly good! Well, to our onions; you must be starving – go to lunch.' Lisa retired to the changing room and having replaced Lisette on the hanger went to sit for the free time remaining in Hyde Park. If Lisette were to be reduced to fifty guineas she would have almost enough money in her Post Office money box to pay for it. The thought of spending this sum, which was very much more than she had ever had at her disposal before and sufficient for at least ten ordinary frocks at the usual retail prices, was utterly intoxicating.

47

During all these days of Patty's dislocation, even grief, her colleagues had been much too busy, first with Christmas and then with the sales, to notice the change in her demeanour. She was, as Joy had remarked, a pale creature at the best of times, and if her usual desultory chatter with its liberal if unenlightening references to her husband had ceased, the occasion for it had in any case vanished: customers and their servicing had swallowed up every available moment. Throughout this period Patty had worked on doggedly, but at the end of each day she succumbed to an exhaustion which overwhelmed and even frightened her. Her appetite had all but disappeared; she dined off slices of cold ham and tomatoes, and drank cups of strangely milkless tea. Do I feel tired because I feel sick, she wondered, or do I feel sick because I feel tired?

Just try not to worry, said Dawn. He'll come back. Well, she wasn't worrying, no she wasn't: she felt now too tired and too sick to worry about Frank. She wasn't even angry any longer. She needed all her thoughts for herself at the moment, because she simply had to keep going as best she could: had to go in to Goode's, and get through the day, and come home and get ready for the next one. Look, just try and forget about him, said Joy, at least until he turns up again: buy some new clothes, and take a holiday. Go to Bateman's Bay with Dawn, haven't you got holidays due? Enjoy yourself for a bit. Come to the beach with us on Sunday, we thought we might make a day of it and go up to Manly, go on. Oh, she was so tired. I'll see, she said. I'll let you know. I'll ring you on Saturday.

Come and stay with me, said Mrs Crown. It'll be like old times. You can leave a note for Frank! But she just wanted to be left alone. She didn't want to have to pretend anything: when you're alone, you needn't pretend, need you? Although, of course, sometimes you do: sometimes the lies you tell yourself are worse than the ones you tell other people. Now how can that be?

44

They had seen a film at the Savoy, with sub-titles which Fay soon found perfectly easy to read while continuing to watch the actors although she never would have expected it, and as it was the most heart-breaking story she had a job to prevent herself from crying which would have made her look an awful fool and moreover would have ruined her eye make-up; and now they were in a little restaurant at King's Cross where the food was quite delicious and where Rudi seemed to know a lot of the other diners, waving and bowing to right and left as people came and went. The strangest thing of all was that Rudi was so terribly easy to talk to. There was no need to hide a thing.

'So you have never seen a French film before? My God, I see I have arrived here just in time. We will see them all, *Les Enfants*, *Les Jeux*, *La Regie*, *Le Jour*. Etcetera. It will take forever, we will have time for almost nothing else. Well, there is no opera here and virtually no theatre so the time we have. I will get the programme of the University Film Soc as soon as the academic year begins, they show them all the time, so they did anyway in Melbourne. Of course anyone may walk in there, why not? Taste some of this veal, it is very good here.

'Yes, I was a bureaucrat in Budapest – what a line! I should write a song! – a statistician. Shall I tell you what that is? Here, I intend to make money – what else? I did not escape into the capitalist west in order to work for a salary for the rest of my life. Oh, there is a fortune to be made here by anyone with a reasonable knowledge of economic statistics and a little imagination – several fortunes. My friends are doing it all the time and they have no knowledge even of statistics. You see, the country is underdeveloped and the population must also be increased as quickly as feasible. So I intend to become rich, myself; I will be doing a favour to everybody. Tell me, do you prefer Brahms to Beethoven or Tchaikovsky to both? *You are not sure?* Well. I will take care of that too if you will permit me. You have such musicality or you could not dance so well. No, I am quite serious. This is a serious matter. So you are reading *Anna K*, are you – ah, so Lisa lent it to you. Remarkable. Well, life is, fortunately, long, even though not as long as art, so you have plenty of time to finish it and go on to the rest. You are already extremely well-read for a dancer. But now I think it is time for me to shut up, as they say, because you are ready for the dessert and I have not yet finished this, so while I do so I think you had better tell me the story of your life. Begin at the beginning! Who was your father?'

And Fay began to tell, for the first time ever, the story of her life, and as it became quite a sad story quite soon – for her father had been killed in the war when Fay was eleven years old and her elder brother fifteen, and this misfortune had been extended in its consequences through a series of poor choices and contrivances on the part of Fay's well-meaning but not very competent mother – Rudi brought it to a temporary halt at the point where

Fay left school at the unwisely early moment of her sixteenth birthday, and called for the dessert menu. 'It is time for you now to eat something very sweet and tasty,' he said; 'I can recommend the chocolate pudding here, it is formidable. Let me digest the story so far before you give me the next chapter. I had not imagined you to have such a tale to tell – you Australians are mysterious people, no one would guess that this is a place where people can also suffer. It is the constant sunshine, it hides everything but itself.'

Fay was glad to stop talking for the time being, for oddly enough she now found that her tale was affecting her too: she had almost been on the point of tears at one or two moments. 'Listen,' said Rudi, 'let me tell you a Hungarian joke. Let me see, I must translate.' She laughed so much that tears – now – came into her eyes. How sweet she is, thought Rudi. A nice healthy Australian girl, just as I commanded, but with a tragic tale withal. What a lucky bastard I am. Then he had, uncharacteristically, a twinge of doubt. Does she like me? he wondered. I'll have to be careful. He did hope that she did for, if she did, he thought it quite possible that he might actually decide to marry her. 'What would you like to do tomorrow night?' he asked. 'Shall we see if there is a concert programme which appeals? I'll look at the *Herald* in the morning and telephone you in the afternoon. Well, your landlady will have to put up with it – I will smother her in Middle European charm, don't worry, she will soon be looking forward to my telephone calls, she will not mind the disturbance at all.' He's so *nice*, thought Fay. I never knew men could be so nice. What on earth does he see in me? She wasn't even trying any more, she was simply swept along on the tide of Rudi's energy and charm. It was the most entirely novel, and the most blissful, sensation.

45

'Stefan, please be entirely frank with me. Do you think I am too fat in this costume?' Magda posed herself attractively in the bedroom doorway, one hand placed on a well-rounded hip, the other gracefully resting against the jamb; she was wearing a two-piece swimming costume made of a white material with large dark red flowers printed on it. 'No, no, not for a minute,' Stefan assured her. He was reading the Sunday papers, such as they were, waiting for Magda to be ready. 'Stefan, please be serious,' said Magda. 'Tell me what you really think.' 'I have done so,' said Stefan, 'I was never more serious in my life. You are not too fat in that costume.' 'Not too fat,' said Magda, 'but fat, yes?' '*No*,' said Stefan, 'not in fact fat at all.' 'I suppose you mean plump,' said Magda. 'I am beginning to wish I had never been born,' said Stefan. 'Yes, I know what you mean,' said Magda. 'I feel like this when my own husband will not give me his frank opinion. It is little enough to ask.'

'My frank opinion, for the last time, is that the costume and the person inside it look perfectly okay. So could you collect your necessities now and let us be off, for I must say that if we are not on our way within five minutes I believe I shall go quite mad.'

Magda turned with a sigh and he heard her clattering about. She re-emerged in a dark blue one-piece costume over which she had thrown a beach robe. 'I like you in that costume too,' Stefan said, 'almost as much as the other.' Magda clucked. 'Let us go, then,' she said. 'I do not want to see you go mad.'

They argued about whether they would go to Bilgola or to Whale Beach, and decided at last on the latter just as they were approaching the former, but at last they were settled under their umbrella with their towels and cushions, books and picnic basket, in time for a swim before lunch. After the swim they argued no more; the blue Pacific had washed away all their irritation, as it generally does.

While they were eating their cold chicken Magda said, 'Have you noticed something strange? We have heard nothing from Rudi this weekend. I wonder why.' 'Well, he is obviously engaged elsewhere,' said Stefan. 'No, but *where?*' asked Magda. 'Oh, good heavens, how should I know? There is any number of possibilities,' said Stefan. 'I would not have thought so,' said Magda. 'I see only one.' 'And what could that be?' asked Stefan, incredulously. 'Well, did you not see who he left the party with?' said Magda. 'No,' said Stefan, 'I did not notice. Rudi I think always leaves a party with a girl, usually the prettiest – but I did not see him go.' 'I did,' said Magda. 'He left with *Fay*. He was taking her home.' 'That is the least he could do,' said Stefan, 'after you had gone to the trouble of asking her, a nice healthy Australian girl, just for his benefit. Didn't he say he wanted to marry such a one? So it would seem perfectly in order for him to take her home after the party, to say nothing of for the rest of her life. He must begin somewhere. They are probably married by now, come to think of it – the party is almost a week ago.'

'Oh do be serious,' said Magda. 'How can you joke about such a matter? If Rudi is indeed with Fay now, if he is continuing to see her, then I feel I should know of it. I feel responsible.' 'And well you might,' said Stefan. 'I thought it was you who were not serious, when you proposed inviting her in order to accommodate Rudi.' 'Well, I was and I wasn't,' said Magda. 'I was half-serious. But no more. Whereas, if Rudi is seeing her, then the thing becomes more than half-serious, and I feel my responsibility.' 'I do not see why you worry,' said Stefan. 'She is an adult, after all. She can look after herself.' 'I don't know,' said Magda. 'Rudi is rather a wolf, I believe. She is a naïve Australian girl, experienced no doubt only with clumsy Australian men. I wonder whether she can deal with someone like Rudi.' 'Oh, what is this fuss,' said Stefan. 'He cannot harm her. He is probably a very amusing companion for her. She is probably having the time of her life.' 'So long as she does not get her heart broken,' said Magda darkly. 'It will be my fault if she does.' 'Oh, do not dramatise,' said Stefan. 'They will live happily ever after, and have many fine children, they will ask you to be the godmother, and will be in your debt forever for having introduced them to each other.'

'Do not joke, I implore you,' said Magda: 'you know perfectly well that such a match is quite impossible. Rudi, and Fay! I only thought he might amuse himself a little at the party with his healthy Australian girl – and she dances very well, did you see? She told me she had been for a while a professional – that is all. I did not take his idea of marrying seriously, I did not think he meant me to do so. But if he is taking her out now – well, that I would not have expected. What can they have in common? He will break her heart yet, you will see.' 'This is melodrama,' said

Stefan. 'The reality is that both are at a loose end, it suits them both for the time being to see each other, that is all. Look! I am almost as bad as you – we do not know if they are in fact seeing each other at all. Rudi may be amusing himself at this moment with someone quite different.'

'No, I feel he is with Fay,' said Magda portentously, 'and I hope that there is only amusement, on each side. But she is a woman, although an Australian, so you know it is never after all only amusement, on the part of a woman. The heart is always engaged, and so may be broken. And it will be my fault.' 'I think you are crossing the bridge before the horse has bolted,' said Stefan. 'It is time for another swim. Come along!'

'I should have telephoned Magda and Stefan this weekend,' said Rudi. 'I have seen them so often; they will think my silence odd. I will do it later perhaps.' He and Fay were sitting on a large towel on Tamarama beach eating sandwiches provided by Fay: there were two rounds filled with peanut butter and celery, and two with cheddar cheese and lettuce. Rudi was charmed. 'So these are Australian sandwiches, are they?' he asked. 'I suppose they must be,' said Fay. Are they different from Continental sandwiches?' 'I will make you some one of these days,' Rudi assured her, 'and you will see.' He ate another, pensively, tasting the flavour of the country. There was fruit to eat afterwards and then Fay read some more *Anna* while Rudi looked about him, sizing up the young women and making mental notes on the behaviour of the families in the vicinity.

He was fairly sure that the forthcoming chapter of Fay's life story would contain details which she might feel some shame in divulging, for if ever there were a girl who had, according to the code of the time and place, fallen, however inadvertently, then Fay was likely to be that girl. The thing was to elicit the details as quickly and painlessly as possible, to reassure her, and to pass on swiftly to the tale's conclusion which must thereafter be nigh. Then, after delivering a somewhat edited account of his own amours, he could at last begin to prepare the ground for a possible proposal of marriage. What a time these things took!

'I have decided to live in the Eastern suburbs, by the way,' he remarked. 'The North Shore is very pretty but it is too far away. And on this side there is more bustle, it is more like city than suburban life. So I am going to look seriously for a flat this week – I prefer Bellevue Hill but it is so expensive; perhaps I will try Rose Bay or Vaucluse. What do you think?' 'Well, they're all nice,' said Fay, wonderingly. Rudi was talking about the posh side of the Eastern suburbs: well, he had announced his intention of making lots of money: perhaps he would begin to do it soon. Oh, how frightened she felt. Here she was, with an extraordinary man, so kind, so understanding, so funny, and attractive too, and determined to be rich into the bargain, and why he was interested in her was an entire mystery: but the point was, that soon – for she was sure she could not conceal these episodes – he would learn about Mr Marlow and Mr Green, and that would very likely be that. In the midst of the blissful sensation which Rudi's attentions to her had induced she felt the sudden sharp bite of fear. My life is wrecked, she thought; she put down her book and looked out at the sea.

'A penny for your thoughts!' said Rudi. 'Oh, nothing,' said Fay sadly. 'Tonight, when we are having dinner,' said Rudi, 'for that is what we shall do tonight if you are free – yes? – good – you will tell me the rest of your story. Or would you rather tell it to me now?' 'No,' said Fay. 'I'll wait until tonight.' It will be easier with something to drink, she thought. 'After that it will be my turn to tell you about my own *disgraceful* past,' said Rudi. 'You will probably not want to know me after you have heard the tale!' Fay looked at him uncertainly, and then they smiled at each other. Rudi leaned over and kissed her cheek. She suddenly realised that everything was going to be quite all right. 'It's time for another swim,' Rudi said. 'Come along!'

46

Patty opened her eyes to the new day, and remembering, despaired. For two pins she would have stayed where she was forever. But that wouldn't do; she must keep going; at least it was Monday again and her duties were plain; there were no dreadful acres of empty time to fill: it was time to rise and get ready for work. She sat up and climbed out of bed, but as her feet touched the floor she was seized by a sudden feeling of quite awful nausea, and she sat rigid until it passed. Then gingerly she stood up and went into the bathroom.

She managed to wash and dress but shortly after putting the bread into the toaster she found the horrible sick sensation seizing her once more, and this time so violently that she ran into the bathroom and threw up. Oh Jesus, she thought, what is happening to me? It can't be. It must be something I ate yesterday at Manly. It was the meat pie, that's what it was. I knew I shouldn't.

She felt quite dazed, here at Goode's, with the second week of the sales at full throttle all around her. I should look at the swimming cossies in my lunch hour, she thought. Maybe I should get some new clothes, too, like Joy keeps saying. Splash out. But she felt so sick, so weak, that when her lunch hour came she could do no more than retire to the canteen. Fay didn't accompany her. 'I'm going to change and then look over the sales things,' said she brightly. 'I need some new clothes!' Oh yes, thought Patty bitterly. Make hay while the sun shines. She felt dreadful, sitting in the canteen with a cup of tea and a salad sandwich from which she had taken only one bite.

'Off your food? that's no good!' cried a sharp voice, and its owner sat down suddenly in the chair next to hers. 'Oh hello, Paula,' said Patty wanly. 'How's the nightie?' asked Paula, with a vaguely suggestive smirk. Patty tried to smile. 'Oh, it's fine,' she said. 'It's really nice. I should have bought two.' 'Yes, I *told* you,' said Paula. 'They've all gone now so you're too late. Still, we're getting new stock in a fortnight so you should pay us another visit, you might see something else as good.' 'Yes, I will,' said Patty. She was desperate. Paula's question, the conversation which followed, were terrible reminders of her situation and its prelude. But a brilliant light suddenly at this moment flashed on in her mind. She had never previously quite seen that the night of the black nightdress and Frank's disappearance, the one event following so hard upon the other, might in fact be connected in some way.

A vast area of speculation was revealed but where she was to begin to speculate she did not know. She had never had to think in such a manner before and did not know how it was to be done; she knew only that the possibility of a connection was placed before her, and that if the connection were to be established, she might then know something about the reason for Frank's disappearance. But all opportunity for further thought was snatched away by Paula who continued to chatter brightly until it was time for Patty to return to Ladies' Cocktail. The burning desert of the long afternoon now stretched before her.

Shortly after three o'clock Lisa noticed a weatherbeaten-looking man hovering about on the edge of the Ladies' Cocktail section and she took particular note of him for the three very good reasons that, one, it was excessively rare to see a man (other than Mr Ryder) on this floor at all, and two, that if one were to see a man (other than Mr Ryder) here it would be a Rudi-ish sort of man, and not, three, someone who looked like one of the strange bipeds to be seen in the vicinity of the Hotel Australia during the week of the Sheep Show. I wonder if I should ask him what he wants, she thought. He must be lost.

Fay noticed the man at just this moment. 'Gee, look at that,' she said in a low murmur to Lisa. 'He's a long way from home!' The two began to giggle and this sound alerted Miss Jacobs. 'Now, you two,' she said, 'save your laughter until after hours. I can't see what's so funny about this section at the moment. Haven't you got better things to do? There's Patty doing all the putting-away. You see if you can't help her while we've got a few moments to ourselves.' The two young women turned away to do her bidding but a customer approached as they did so and Fay remained at the counter to take her money. Lisa took a step towards the rail where Patty was replacing some frocks which had been tried on and found wanting but at this instant the man, whom she had managed (intrigued as she mightily was) to keep in her sights all the while, began to come nearer. He seemed to be approaching Lisa herself – how odd! – perhaps he wanted help after all; perhaps he wished to buy a frock for his wife and wanted advice for which he had only now found the courage to ask. As Lisa reached the rail of frocks, Patty, who had had her back towards both Lisa and the strange weather-beaten man, turned around.

No sooner had she done so – it was true that she was looking very pale, Lisa had noticed it herself – than she suddenly fell in a heap on the floor, with a ghastly thud which itself made Lisa start with a shock. 'Oh!' cried the girl. 'She's fainted!' And she felt so shocked that she even began to tremble. Oh, what was she to do? There was Patty, stretched out on the floor in her black frock, as white as a sheet, with the cocktail frocks which had been draped over her arm all tumbled around and about her: and the remarkable thing was, that all the while the ridiculous man was still standing near by, doing nothing, and staring down at Patty.

'She's fainted,' said Lisa to the man. 'I'm just going to get some help.' 'I know,' said the man. 'She's my wife.'

Lisa stared at him. Good heavens, what on earth was going on? 'Well, I'll just get Miss Jacobs,' she said. 'She'll know what to do.' She went to fetch Miss Jacobs. 'Mrs Williams has fainted,' she said. Miss Jacobs threw up her hands. 'Go and tell Mr Ryder,' she said. 'He'll telephone up for the nurse.' She hurried over to inspect her colleague. Miss Jacobs now saw the strange man. 'If you'll excuse me,' she said with some sarcasm and much dignity, 'I must attend to this lady who has fainted.' 'I know,' said Frank, again. 'She's my wife.' 'Gracious me,' said Miss Jacobs. 'Well, it's fortunate you're here then. Even if you ought not to be. She'll need someone to take her home. The nurse is on her way. Has she been ill lately?' 'I don't know,' said Frank. 'I've been away.' 'Oh, have you?' said Miss Jacobs. 'I see.' She pursed her lips.

Magda now appeared, like a crested eagle in a barnyard: she had viewed the greater part of the scene so far. 'I have some sal volatile,' she cried. 'There is nothing like it!' She flourished a phial. Miss Jacobs had managed to collect and hang up the fallen cocktail frocks and to loosen Patty's clothing so far as was consistent with decency, and by supporting her with one arm around her shoulders, to raise her up to a half-sitting position. Magda held the sal volatile under Patty's nose, and Patty opened her eyes and sat up with a great start.

The first sight which met her awakened gaze was Frank, and

she stared at him for one abominable instant. Then she spoke. 'Go to hell,' she said.

'Now, you've had a shock,' said Miss Jacobs. 'You just be quiet. The nurse is coming. You're not well.' She turned to Frank. 'Perhaps you'd better wait somewhere out of the way,' she said. 'Go out onto the fire stairs, we'll send for you when she can be taken home.'

'Tell him to go to hell,' said Patty.

'Now, now,' said Miss Jacobs. Frank at last opened his mouth and spoke. 'I've been to hell,' he said: 'I've just come back. But I didn't have me key. I just came here to get the front door key from you, that's all.'

'Oh God,' said Patty. 'Oh Jesus. I should have known.' And she began to cry. The nurse now arrived. 'What's all this?' she said. 'Let me see the patient.' She began to take Patty's pulse and to ask questions. Frank lingered near the door to the fire stairs. 'She'd better go home then if her husband's here,' said the nurse. 'Now you mind you see your doctor tonight if you're still feeling faint. Someone should go to the locker room with her while she changes.' Lisa was assigned this unhappy task and when she at last returned to Ladies' Cocktail it was business as usual: Miss Cartright had helped to hold the fort and told her underlings that they could send for her again if they should find themselves too short-handed during Mrs Williams's absence. 'She'll be here again in the morning with any luck,' she said. 'It's probably just the heat, and not eating a proper lunch. I always tell you girls but some of you won't listen. Eat a proper lunch!' She sailed away in a flutter of black and white stripes. This is not like Mrs Williams, she thought. Fainting, on the second floor! It really won't do. Still, that's the sales for you: the end of the week can't come too soon, I can tell *you*!

47

'Patty Williams fainted this afternoon,' said Lisa. 'Good heavens! what, in Goode's?' 'Yes, right in the middle of Ladies' Cocktail,' said Lisa. 'Her husband was there too.' 'Her husband? but what was *he* doing there?' asked Mrs Miles, astonished. 'I don't know,' said Lisa. 'Fay and I had to look after the section while Miss Jacobs was with Patty and the nurse so we didn't hear what was going on. All I know is, that –' and she recounted the events which she herself had witnessed. 'Well, that all sounds very odd to me,' said Mrs Miles. 'Fancy him turning up there like that. And then her fainting. Goodness me. Don't you go fainting, now. Do you eat a proper lunch when you forget to take your sandwiches? Promise me. You see what can happen if you don't. She ought to know better at her age. Poor thing. I wonder why she hasn't had any children.' 'You should see her husband!' cried Lisa. 'Now Lesley, what do you know about that?' asked her mother. 'Well, he's completely gormless,' said Lisa. 'So are lots of men,' said Mrs Miles. 'It doesn't stop them from becoming fathers.'

Now that fathers had been mentioned the related subject of Lisa's future was brought before them: it could hardly be avoided. The distractions of Christmas and the New Year were behind them and Lisa's fate was very nearly in view: the Leaving Certificate examination results were to be published at the end of the week. They would appear in the Saturday editions of the *Herald* and the *Telegraph*; a large number of the examinees would go and inspect them on the proof-sheets of the first editions, which were posted for the purpose outside the newspaper offices late on Friday evening. It might have been thought that Lisa's father, privy much sooner still to the vital information, could have passed it on earlier in the day but so delicate was the subject of these results and the prohibited ambition which depended upon them that the subject had not been mentioned in his presence. He himself had expressed no interest in it whatsoever.

'I suppose you'll go down to the *Herald* on Friday night to see the results,' said Mrs Miles in a matter-of-fact tone. 'Oh, yes, probably,' Lisa agreed with an air of equal unconcern. 'I might as well.' Mrs Miles could see nothing for it but to allude directly to the question which was now so immediate. 'If you've done very well,' she said, 'if you're pretty sure to get that scholarship, then I think it might be a good idea if we let your father stew for a few days after the results come out. I know he's very stubborn about you not going to the university but all the same, it might be a good idea to let him stew. There's plenty of time to try and talk him around before you'd have to enrol.' 'Oh, I suppose so,' said Lisa unhappily. She could hardly endure the idea of further waiting, further uncertainty. 'There's a few more weeks before the scholarship list is announced anyway,' Mrs Miles pointed out. 'Just let him stew. You can wait.' 'And if I don't get good results,' said Lisa, 'there's nothing to worry about anyway.' 'No,' said Mrs Miles. 'But you will.' And she knew this for a fact, she felt it in her bones. 'Don't you worry, Lesley,' she said; '*Lisa.* Everything will work out. You'll see. You just make sure you eat properly. Eat a proper lunch; don't go fainting like that Mrs Williams. What was that stuff you wanted me to try and get for your sandwiches like you had at Magda's? Salami? Well, I'll see if I can find any. I suppose there's some salami somewhere in Chatswood. I'll have a good look tomorrow. Salami. I'll write it down so I don't forget.'

48

They went home to Randwick in a taxi, sitting side by side in complete silence, and then Patty found her front door key and they stepped across the threshold. Frank followed his wife into the kitchen and sat down awkwardly on a chair; she filled the electric jug and switched it on. While she waited for it to boil she studied the charming picture on the packet of Billy Tea, of a man sharing a cup of tea with a kangaroo. They were a more congenial couple than she and Frank, that was quite certain. This reflection was almost funny: she half-realised that the whole situation was almost funny. 'Where have you been?' she asked, quite calmly.

'Wagga,' said Frank.

Patty though for a moment. 'Wagga?' she said. '*Wagga!*' 'Phil O'Connell,' said Frank. 'Who used to work at Wonda. Came into some money and bought a pub there. You remember. He was always asking me to go down, at first. So I went to have a look. Gave him a hand over Christmas and the New Year – there's lots of extra trade then.' 'You never thought to tell me of course,' said Patty. 'I'm only your wife. I wouldn't worry, would I? I wouldn't be wondering what had happened or anything, would I? I wouldn't have to tell lies for you at Wonda Tiles or spend two weeks feeling sick and terrible and then have you just turning up at Goode's like that, I don't know how I'll ever show my face there again. I don't even know why you've come back here now. I suppose you ran out of clean shirts, did you? Well you can sort out your own bloody shirts from now on. I've had enough!' And she burst into tears and ran into the bedroom.

Frank followed her and stood in the doorway wondering what to do. She was lying on the bed, crying, with her face pressed into the pillow. At last he came over and sat down heavily on the side of the bed. He touched her shoulder. 'I'm sorry,' he said. 'I never thought of all that.' 'Well you're stupid then!' cried Patty. 'Stupid and selfish!'

'Yes, I suppose that's right,' said Frank. 'I have been.' He thought about this for a time. 'I should have thought,' he said. 'I had my mind on other things.' 'Like what, for instance?' asked Patty. 'I dunno,' said Frank. 'I just felt – well – after that night – you know – I thought you wouldn't want to see me again. For a while.' '*You* thought!' cried Patty. 'You thought that, did you? You're lying. It's you didn't want to see *me*, that's more like it!' And as she said this, she knew it was true: and it was something she had not known at all, had not even suspected: it had just come into her mind, just now, as Frank had spoken. Frank looked down at the floor and Patty saw the shame and confusion on his face. She felt not tenderness or sympathy, but a sort of resignation. Oh God: her mother had been right: men were children, who did not understand themselves, and could not. Frank suddenly looked at her. 'I'll make it up to you,' he said. 'I promise.' 'Oh, yeah,' said Patty. 'We'll see, won't we?' And suddenly the future looked, as it had not done for years and years, interesting. She sat up. 'I'm that hungry,' she said. 'Could you go down the street and get us some fish and chips? I'll just ring Mum while you're out, she's been that worried about you. Don't be long; I'm *starving*.'

49

'Honestly, Joy, I can't see what's so *funny*, Patty must—' 'Oh Dawn, for God's sake, can't you? It's the funniest thing I've heard for years! Frank buggers off like that without a word, then turns up two weeks later in the middle of the Ladies' Cocktail at Goode's because he's lost his, front door key – it's priceless! Wait till I tell Dave!'

'You don't have to make a comedy out of it, Joy. You wouldn't be laughing if it happened to you. You never think of what Patty's gone through.' 'More fool Patty. Well, maybe she'll know better now. It's time she sharpened her wits. I wouldn't have had him back, not at any price!' 'Yes, well, you're not Patty like I keep saying. And that reminds me, how did she look to you on Sunday? Did she look sick or anything? I mean it's not like her to *faint*. She says she's not going in to work today, she's not feeling a hundred percent. She's going to the doctor. I don't like the sound of that.'

'Oh, she's all right, she was her usual self on Sunday, didn't say much, didn't do much, sat on the beach with the papers and that. She'll brighten up now that Frank's back, ha ha ha.' 'Well, maybe she'll have a break, maybe she'll take some sick leave, have a rest for a while. She's had a bad time, she needs a break. You just mind your tongue when you talk to her, she hasn't got your sense of humour.'

'Yes, that's her problem, isn't it? Well, maybe she'll learn. She'd better, if she's going to stick with Frank. Oh God, what a story. Didn't have his key! If only that was the only thing he didn't have!' 'Honestly, Joy,' said Dawn. 'You're *awful*.'

Miss Cartright came swishing over to Ladies' Cocktail and having cast an expert eye over the remaining sale items on their rail she beckoned to Lisa. 'We've just heard from Mrs Williams,' she told her. 'She saw her doctor yesterday and the result is that she will be away for the rest of this week and the whole of next. As you know, this was to have been your last week with us but it would be a great help if you could come in next week to cover for Mrs Williams because although the sales finish this week, thank goodness, there'll be lots to do next week with the new stock going out. You'll have to work like a slave. Are you game?' 'Gosh,' said Lisa, delighted. 'Of course!' 'Jolly good,' said Miss Cartright. 'That's settled then. I'll be helping out here during this week if you find yourselves short-handed. I'll just go and speak to Miss Jacobs so that we all know where we are.' She swished away. Lisa could not wait until lunchtime: she ran across the carpet and entered Magda's pink-lit cave. 'Magda!' she said in an urgent whisper. 'Is it still here?' Magda understood her instantly. 'Yes,' she said. 'It is still here.' 'It's sold,' said Lisa. 'Very good,' said Magda. 'I will put it aside for you.'

She returned during her lunch hour after having changed. 'Ah, Mademoiselle Miles,' said Magda, beaming. 'You have come to collect your frock, yes? It is ready for you – shall I pack it or did you wish to try it on once more?' 'Oh Magda – I'm sorry – I can't take it away today, I haven't any money with me. I won't have all the money until tomorrow week – you see I'm working next week as well to cover for Patty Williams while she's sick.' 'Ah yes,' said Magda. 'I see. Well it is not the usual thing in here but for so distinguished a customer I make an exception. I will put it away in the alterations cupboard until next week. Oh, by the way' – she took Lisette, the rustling white and scarlet-spotted fantasy of young girlhood, from its padded hanger and shook it out so that its flounces floated once and sighed back down again – 'Miss Cartright has been in here this morning. All our white dresses, this and two others, are a little further reduced. With the staff discount, Lisette is now exactly thirty-five guineas. We are giving it away.' 'Oh,' exclaimed Lisa, 'that's absolutely wonderful!' She counted the contents of her money box in her head: after paying for Lisette she would actually have some change.

50

'Jánosi?' said Myra. 'How do you spell it?' Fay told her. 'Well,' said Myra. 'It takes a bit of getting used to. But he could change it, you know. Quite a few of them do that.' 'Rudi won't,' said Fay. 'Rudi says the best thing to do when there's anything unusual about you is to brazen it out.' 'Oh, does he?' said Myra. 'Well, that's one way I suppose. Especially if you've got a thick skin.' Fay bridled. 'Rudi is the most sensitive man I ever knew,' she said. 'Okay, don't get shirty,' said Myra. 'I didn't mean to be offensive. I just think—' she broke off and looked wildly into the space beyond Fay's right shoulder.

They were drinking iced coffee in Repin's, and then Fay was going to meet Rudi, and Myra was going to her club. What did Myra think? It was difficult to articulate and more difficult still to enunciate. Myra was in a state of mild shock, that was all. Fay! Swept off her feet, by a Hungarian reffo with an impossible surname, whom Myra had not even met, whose motives she darkly suspected. What was he after? This would end in tears, make no mistake! And the only obstruction between Fay and a horrid disaster was she, Myra: but how to save the silly creature, when she could hear no word of criticism of this Rudi Jánosi – when she had great blinding stars in her eyes? Oh, God give me strength, thought Myra. What can I do?

'*What* do you think?' asked Fay. 'Oh, I dunno,' said Myra. 'It's just that – well, you haven't known him long, you don't know anything about him really – you don't – I don't want to see you get hurt.' 'I'd rather get hurt by Rudi than by the types I used to know,' said Fay. Myra was inclined to take umbrage at this: those types were her types. But she was fair-minded; she saw Fay's point, even if she didn't want to grant it. 'At least with an Australian you know where you are,' she said huffily. 'Oh maybe,' said Fay, 'but it's not so hot if you don't want to be there anyway. At least with a Continental you're going somewhere new.' 'Yes, but it might be dangerous,' said Myra. 'You might get hurt.' They had gone around in a circle, it was hopeless. But what had happened to Fay in ten brief days? 'Yes I might,' she said. 'It might be dangerous. But life is dangerous.' Ye gods! 'Life is dangerous.' Where did she get that from? 'You should hear some of Rudi's stories. Then you'd know. We live in a cocoon here. That's what he says. We don't know how lucky we are.' 'Well, I suppose *he* does,' said Myra. 'Oh yes,' said Fay. 'He knows how lucky he is; he never stops saying so.'

Myra felt suddenly helpless; she gave up the struggle. 'Do you love him?' she said. 'Yes,' said Fay, 'I reckon I do.' She smiled. She had not quite dared to say this yet even to herself, and to say it now was to push open a heavy door which had concealed a great sunlit garden where she was now suddenly free to wander. 'But don't tell *anyone*,' she said to Myra. 'It's our secret, okay? Because you're my best friend.' 'Right you are, Fay,' said Myra. Oh God, she thought, I hope this is going to work out for the kid. She's had a lot of bad luck so far. Please let this one be okay, even though he is a Continental. And she crossed her fingers hard on the hand which Fay couldn't see.

51

This morning it was Lisa who felt sick because today was the day which preceded the night when she would discover how well or how ill she had succeeded in the Leaving Certificate examinations. She had a whole day at Goode's to endure, and several more hours thereafter – she would go to see a film – before it was time to go down to the *Herald* or the *Telegraph* and discover the worst. Her stomach was already in a state of turmoil. 'I can't eat a thing,' she said to her mother, and the latter for once did not insist.

Just after Mr Miles arrived at his place in the composing room late in the afternoon one of his colleagues came over to him. 'Hey, Ed,' he said, 'haven't you got a daughter who's just done the Leaving? They've finished setting the results. Go and have a look. Put the kid out of her misery.' Ed Miles was in a grump. 'Nah,' he said. 'Let her sweat. *She* wanted to do the Leaving. I told her it was a waste of time but she and her mother wouldn't listen. I haven't got time for looking at results, I've got work to do.' 'Ah, come on,' said his colleague. 'Don't be a spoilsport. It's a big day for her. What school was she?' Mr Miles informed him grudgingly. Five minutes later his colleague returned. 'Hey, Ed,' he said, 'is her name Lesley? Right. Listen to this.' He had a slip of paper. He read out a list of results which as even Mr Miles could see were rather impressive. There was a brief silence while Mr Miles continued to all appearances to carry on with his work. At last he spoke. 'That sounds all right, doesn't it?' he said. 'Thanks.' 'Geez, Ed,' said his colleague, 'you're a cool one. It's bloody good, that's what. You should be celebrating.' 'Well I'm not,' said Mr Miles. 'I've got work to do, so leave me to get on with it.' 'Gee whiz,' said his colleague. 'You bet.' He went away and regaled the rest of the crew with the tale of Ed Miles's phlegm in the face of his daughter's brilliance.

The night editor now came in; he sauntered over to Ed Miles. 'I hear your daughter's distinguished herself famously,' he said. 'Congratulations! Wonderful news! I suppose she'll be off to the university in the new term? You must be proud.' 'Well, I don't know about that,' said Mr Miles. 'I don't know about *the university*.' 'Oh, surely!' exclaimed the night editor. 'You can't waste brains like that. She'll have a wonderful time. And you tell her to come and see us if she wants a cadetship – first-class honours in English, she must know how to write. Yes, university's the thing – mine are both there now, they're having the time of their lives. You tell her from me, she can't do anything better at her age!' He sauntered away again. Eventually Mr Miles got so fed up with his workmates coming over and shaking his hand and congratulating him that he acceded to their irritating expectations by going and telephoning home. His daughter was of course absent; he spoke to his wife. 'Just thought I might as well tell you Lesley's results,' he said; 'if you want to know. I've got 'em here.' He read them out to her. She gasped, and burst into tears. 'This is the happiest day of my life,' she said. 'Can't you come home early? She should be back soon.' 'Can't really,' he said. 'I'll see youse tomorrow. Got to go now.' He hung up.

Lisa thought of ringing her mother but there were so many others queuing for the nearest public telephones for the same purpose that she thought it would be almost as quick simply to go home. She saw some other girls from her school then and they all jumped and squealed together for a minute and pranced away along the street towards downtown and Wynyard Station, chattering disjointedly about their futures, which by the time they entered the station had begun to take on fantastical elements: university life had now fairly begun.

Mrs Miles ran to the door as Lisa opened it: 'Mum!' she cried, her eyes alight, 'I—' 'I know,' said Mrs Miles. 'Your father telephoned.' 'Gosh,' said Lisa. 'What did he say?' 'Nothing much,' said Mrs Miles. 'But you couldn't expect it. He's suffering from shock, or he wouldn't even have phoned. You just let him stew for a bit. You'll see him tomorrow. Don't press him: let it sink in. Oh, Lesley. This is the happiest day of my life!' 'Mine too,' said Lisa, 'so far.' And they laughed and hugged each other and began to cry, and then they danced a jig, and then Mrs Miles made some Milo, because Lisa had to get up in the morning and go to work, exam results or no exam results, and this was no time to be doing without a proper night's sleep, was it?

52

Patty fell backwards onto the unmade bed and lay there exhausted. This made the sixth morning in a row that she had awoken feeling queasy and had soon afterwards had to run into the bathroom and actually throw up. It was also a fact that she was almost two weeks overdue. The possibility which inevitably suggested itself was however too unexpected and, in view of recent events too badly timed, seriously to ponder. But wouldn't it be just like life, she thought, for it to happen now, when Frank – oh, Frank. Here he was.

He stood in the doorway, looking deeply embarrassed. He had been tip-toeing around her ever since his return with an air of terrified circumspection, and as far as Patty was concerned, he could go on doing so. His defection had been papered over, as far as Wonda Tiles was concerned, and he was now back at work after a semi-fictitious malady bearing an impressive Latin name. 'You're damned lucky,' said Patty. 'Another doctor might've left you to take the consequences.' 'I know,' said Frank. 'Don't think I don't appreciate it.' 'Let's see you show it, that's all,' said Patty. She didn't mean to stop tightening the screws just yet, if ever.

'Are you okay?' said Frank in the doorway. 'No,' said Patty. 'I feel bloody.' And so she did. 'Would you like a cup of tea?' 'Yes,' said Patty. 'I'll have it here. I don't feel like getting up just yet. Not too strong. And I'll have some sugar in it.' She lay and looked at the ceiling. After a while Frank came in with a tea tray, and the spectacle it presented almost melted her stern heart. The poor devil was certainly trying. He had found a tray cloth and on it sat the teapot, some milk in a jug and the lump sugar – how had he managed to find that? – in a matching bowl. And from the back of the cutlery drawer he had retrieved the sugar tongs. It was a vision of the genteel tea tray of yesteryear. Oh Lord. Patty sat up. 'That's very nice,' she said. 'I could get used to this.' She sat and sipped the tea.

'When you saw the doctor,' said Frank, 'did you tell him about being sick in the morning?' 'Well maybe I did,' said Patty. 'That's between me and the doctor, isn't it?' She hadn't actually discussed this matter with the doctor, who'd easily been persuaded to give her a chit for some sick leave on the strength of the trial she had lately and so bravely endured. 'Well but,' said Frank, 'what did he say?' 'Never you mind,' said Patty.

'Well –' exclaimed Frank, standing up abruptly and nearly upsetting the tea tray '– I do mind. I *do* mind! I live here too! I am your husband, aren't I? You haven't thrown me out yet. I know I'm not much. I know I'm stupid – well, rather stupid. I never passed any exams. It's all right for you, you had a proper home to grow up in. You don't know what it's like for some of us. I do my best even if it isn't so bloody good. But I do know this. I said I'd make it up to you and I will but I ought to know what's going on. You've been sick every morning since I got back. Are you pregnant?'

Patty was stunned. She put down her teacup. This was the longest speech Frank had ever made; she could hardly begin to take it all in. And now that the word had been uttered, the idea given a real form, she felt suddenly shy and inhibited, and at the same time overjoyed. For it really was possible, even if it was happening at what had seemed to be entirely the wrong time. And all these feelings oddly recalled that night, that saturnalia preceding Frank's weird escapade: she suddenly felt that the secret world they had then entered might not after all be lost to them forever, hidden away and forbidden. She looked at Frank's face and glimpsed in his eyes a pleading and bewildered expression which she had never seen, and was sure she had never aroused, before: she suddenly sensed that he too was remembering that night, and was daring to recollect, if not to acknowledge quite candidly, that realm of wordless and unimaginable intimacy which they had fallen into more or less by accident, whose strangeness had so terrified Frank that he had immediately thereafter vanished into thin air.

Frank came over and sat on the bed once more. 'Please tell me,' he said. 'I've got to know, I've got a right to know, haven't I?' 'Yes,' said Patty. 'I suppose you have. The fact is I'm not sure yet. I might be and I might be not. And it's too soon to find out for certain, I know that. So if I go on like this, I'll visit the doctor in a few weeks and then we'll know. That's all I can say at the moment.' Frank said nothing and Patty suddenly saw that there were tears in his eyes. She sat in silence, and then she touched his hand. 'It'll be our secret for now, okay?' she said. 'Don't say a word.' 'Right you are,' said Frank huskily. Then he took her teacup and put it on the tray, and put the tray on the floor. He lay down beside her and began to caress her, and the entrance to the secret, the wordless and unimaginable, realm suddenly once more gaped hugely before them.

53

Magda was lying in wait at the entrance to the Staff Locker Room. 'Lisa!' she cried, 'I hope your name is also Lesley as your mother called you on the telephone. My young friend, this is a most happy day!' and she kissed her exuberantly on each cheek and held her hands, beaming with pleasure. 'Now your future shines like the sun above you!' she exclaimed. At this moment Fay entered, running rather late. She stopped however on hearing these words. 'What?' she said. 'Is she engaged?' 'Oh tush!' cried Magda. 'At her age? God forbid. No – have you not seen the newspaper? She has obtained magnificent results in the Leaving Certificate. *Mon Dieu*! First class honours, four As, a B, not to be too horribly clever – she is such a good girl! How pleased Stefan and I were – he sends his love of course – we are to have a dinner party for all you clever young people, Michael Foldes had done very well too, did you look? and another girl we also know, so there will be a small celebration soon, I hope next weekend. We will discuss the details later.' 'Gosh,' said Fay; 'gee,

Lisa, that's terrific. Congratulations, I mean it!' Lisa began to be self-conscious because all those standing near by were now taking note and adding their voices. 'Passed the Leaving have you? Good-oh!'

Within a minute of her arrival at Ladies' Cocktail Miss Cartright appeared, and Mr Ryder followed shortly after. 'The world is your oyster,' said the latter; 'mind you don't swallow it whole!' Lisa laughed, but her apprehensions about the approaching encounter with her intransigent father were severe. She was suspended between elation and dread, an almost dreamlike condition. 'Thank you, thank you, thank you,' she kept saying, smiling and smiling. How nice everyone was. Finally the fuss abated and she turned to find something to do so that she might at last efface herself.

'Fay's just told me you've done very well in the examinations,' said Miss Jacobs in a matter of fact tone. 'Is that right? Well, that's no surprise to me at all. I don't expect it's a surprise to you either. You're a clever girl, I could see that. It's a pleasure to work with you and I'll be sorry when you leave us. You'll be going to the university, won't you, of course you will. A clever girl is the most wonderful thing in all Creation you know: you must never forget that. People expect men to be clever. They expect girls to be stupid or at least silly, which very few girls really are, but most girls oblige them by acting like it. So you just go away and be as clever as ever you can: put their noses out of joint for them. It's the best thing you could possibly do, you and all the clever girls in this city and the world. Now, then. We'd better get on and sell some Cocktail Frocks, hadn't we? Yes indeed.'

Lisa wandered about for a while in the half-empty city after leaving Goode's. The afternoon sun lay along the pavements like a benediction: she felt herself still to be in that suspended state and she was dawdling because she did not want to get home before her father awoke. She realised as she walked along George Street that a great barrier had truly been crossed in her life, a barrier greater even than those she had lately crossed, and she felt extremely strange. But to feel strange, she thought, has lately begun to be almost ordinary. Would strangeness increasingly from now on become normality?

Her parents were sitting in the kitchen when she pushed open the back door. Her father rose. 'Well, Lesley,' he said, 'I believe congratulations are in order. Everyone at work sends you theirs too. I've got the night editor and all of them on my back. I can't see what you want with exams and first-class honours and universities and all that when you're a girl. But still. Congratulations. You've done very well.' 'Thanks, Dad,' said Lisa. 'So what do you reckon you'll do now?' said her father. 'You've got to make your own decisions now. You're almost grown up.' 'You know what I want to do now,' said Lisa. 'But you said I couldn't. So I don't know yet.' 'Oh, I suppose you mean the uni,' said her father. 'Yes, well. I'll think about it. That's all. I'll *think* about it. We'll see if you get that scholarship – you won't be going there if you don't. I'm not paying your fees. It's bad enough that I'd have to keep you as long as you're there. So I'll think about it, *if* you get that scholarship. I'll give it careful thought. You needn't celebrate yet. But I'll tell you one thing: if I decide you can go, and you do go, if I ever hear of you being mixed up with any of those libertarians they have there, you're out of this house like a shot and I never want to see you again, is that understood? Right then. If you go, no libertarians, not even *one*.'

Lisa was at last able to catch her mother's eye. They gleamed at each other in secret. The telephone rang. 'You get that, Lisa,' said her mother. 'It's probably that Michael Foldes, he called you earlier.' Lisa returned a few minutes later. 'What did he want?' asked her father suspiciously. Mrs Miles was putting the luncheon on the table: bread, cheese, tomatoes, and a jar of pickles; and some salami which she had indeed managed to find. 'Oh nothing,' said Lisa very calmly. 'He just wanted to know if I was doing anything tonight.' 'Of course you are,' said her father. 'We're all going out to celebrate, aren't we? A slap-up meal at King's Cross or somewhere like that.' 'Yes, that's what I told him,' said Lisa. 'Oh, and he's asked me to go to a dance with him next Saturday week.' 'A dance?' said her mother. 'Where?' 'Oh, the Yacht Squadron,' said Lisa with extreme sang-froid. 'It's being given by the parents of some of his friends at school. It's to celebrate the exam results. They were going to cancel if anyone had failed but no one did, so it's on. Can I go?' 'Well of course,' said her astounded mother. 'But what will you wear?' She felt slightly desperate: a frock suitable for a dance of that kind – well! 'Oh that's all right,' said Lisa. 'There's a frock in the sale at Goode's that will do. I'll buy that.' 'Whatever next?' said her father. 'And who is this bloke? Do I know him?' His wife and daughter reassured him. Mr Miles suddenly felt sad. Lesley had always been there, a kid, not the son he'd wanted, and now suddenly she was going out into the world: now suddenly it was almost all over, and he'd hardly noticed it as it flashed past him. 'Well, enjoy yourself while you can,' he said. 'And what's this?' He picked up a slice of salami. 'That's salami,' said Mrs Miles. 'I got it for Lesley.' 'There's no keeping up with you, Lesley,' said her father. And, he thought, it's true. She's even beginning to look pretty. Filling out. Quite the young lady. Well, what a day it had been. 'Salami, eh,' said Mr Miles, tasting it. 'I suppose I could get used to it. Let me try another piece. Quite tasty. What's it made of?'

54

Fay stood outside the Staff Entrance at closing time on Saturday waiting for Rudi. He was going to keep driving around the block until they coincided; she looked out anxiously to see his elderly Wolseley. There he was. She ran to the kerb and jumped in when he opened the passenger door. 'Full steam ahead!' he said. He was looking pleased with himself, but not insufferably so. 'But where are we going?' asked Fay. 'It's a surprise,' cried Rudi. 'Eat these sandwiches if you're hungry – we haven't time to stop for lunch.'

'Give me a clue,' Fay pleaded. She really hadn't the least idea what might be afoot. 'Here's a clue,' said Rudi, as he turned left. Soon they were driving up William Street, and at last along New South Head Road. 'Oh,' said Fay, as Rushcutter's Bay twinkled beside her, 'I've got it: you've found a flat!' 'Yep,' said Rudi. 'I think I've found one that might do. I want your expert opinion.' 'Me?' said Fay. 'Expert?' 'Absolutely,' said Rudi. 'Now watch out.' They drove through Double Bay and Fay gazed at the Harbour still glittering beside her, past Point Piper, and then a little further along New South Head Road, but at last Rudi turned right into a side street. The car came to a stop outside a pre-war block of flats. 'Now then,' said Rudi; they entered the building and he led the way to the top, which was the third, floor. He took out a key and opened a door, and they walked into the flat.

It was quite empty except for the wallpaper and an 'Early Kooka' gas stove, the old-fashioned kind with a picture of a kookaburra on the oven door. 'It's this which really decided me,' said Rudi, indicating the kookaburra. 'Oh, we used to have one exactly the same at home!' said Fay. 'So,' said Rudi, 'didn't I say you were an expert? Come and look at the rest.' There was a sitting room from which one could just see the Harbour, and two smallish bedrooms. The bathroom was all done in green tiles with a mottled pattern. They went back into the sitting room and looked out of the window. 'See,' said Rudi. 'We could watch the flying boats taking off and landing.' Fay's heart thumped. We? 'Yes,' she said. 'It's lovely.' She dared not ask about whether it might be expensive, or indeed anything else. 'And so handy for the Wintergarden!' said Rudi. 'Not to mention various other amenities. What do you think?' 'Well, I think it's really lovely,' said Fay. 'Like I said. But it's *you* who have to like it, it's your flat. What do *you* think?' 'Oh – I think – listen: will you marry me?' 'I what?' said Fay. She could not believe her ears. What a fool I am, thought Rudi. The question had not been scheduled in quite this way; it had slipped out somewhat before its imagined time. 'Forgive me,' he said. 'I've startled you. I've even startled myself. Let me start – ha! – again, at the beginning. I love you, I adore you, you're sweet, you make me feel happy, I want us to be married as soon as possible if you'll have me – please give me your answer – but think about it for as long as you like: I give you five minutes at least. Shall I leave you alone while you think?'

'No, don't leave me,' said Fay. 'The answer is yes.' 'Thank God for that,' said Rudi. 'We're going to be rich and have lots of children, at least four, is that all right with you?' 'Yes, yes of course,' said Fay. 'I love kids. And money – that always comes in handy.' 'Good,' said Rudi. 'Now –' and he took her in his arms. They had kissed several times but it is a fact that they had been very proper and circumspect and had never approached the margins of unbridled passion. They began now to kiss in a manner which suggested that propriety and circumspection had now had their day, as was quite certainly the case.

Stefan came into the bathroom where Magda was washing her hair. 'That was Rudi on the telephone,' he said. 'Oh?' said Magda. 'He wants to borrow fifty pounds from me,' said Stefan. 'Why?' Magda was very astonished. 'Oh,' said Stefan very casually, 'he wants to buy a diamond ring. Or perhaps a sapphire.' Magda stood up straight, her hair covered in foaming shampoo. 'What are you talking about?' she said. 'Is he going into the jewellery business?' 'I don't believe so,' said Stefan, 'although it could come to that in due course. No, for the moment he wishes only to buy an engagement ring, for Fay.' '*What?*' cried Magda. 'Engagement ring? For *Fay*? What is he thinking of?' 'He is not thinking,' said Stefan. 'He is doing. He and Fay are engaged to be married.' 'This is preposterous,' said Magda. 'Let me rinse my hair.' She did so. Then she wrapped a towel around her head. 'Pour me a whisky,' she said.

They went into the sitting room and sat down with their drinks. The sun was in fact just over the yard-arm: it was after five o'clock. 'I suppose you said you would lend him the money,' said Magda. 'Naturally,' said Stefan. 'How could I stand in his way? Fay is a nice healthy Australian girl.' 'Exactly,' said Magda. 'The whole thing is preposterous. How can they possibly be happy together? They have nothing at all in common.' 'As if that were really a condition for a happy marriage!' said Stefan. 'You are talking like a woman's magazine. The point is they are happy together now. It is the only possible beginning. The middle and end must take care of themselves as they always do. Or not, as the case may be.' Magda thought to herself. 'At least he hasn't after all been trifling with her,' she said. 'At least he isn't breaking her heart as I feared. Although he may do it in the future.' 'Come now,' said Stefan. 'My belief is that he has too much pride to let such a thing occur. He will be a very conscientious husband, you'll see. They both want many children – that will keep them busy: they'll have all that in common. It will be quite enough, you'll see.'

Magda reflected. 'Oh, I suppose so,' she said. 'What the hell. So long as I will not be blamed for anything.' 'You?' said Stefan. 'For introducing them you mean? Don't be idiotic. They are on their own. We can only wish them well. And lend Rudi fifty pounds. Rudi's found a flat, by the way – at Rose Bay. That's why he's short of cash – he has to pay a large deposit.' 'When will they marry?' asked Magda. 'Very soon, as soon as they can arrange it, at the Registry Office probably.' 'Well,' said Magda, 'I do wish them well. With all my heart. But it is still something of a shock.' 'Yes, one's friends can be shocking,' said Stefan. 'It's one of their salient features.' Magda suddenly had a bright idea. 'We were going to have the young people here to dinner next Saturday,' she said, 'to celebrate their examination results: we could make it an engagement celebration as well – what do you think?' 'Yes, why not,' said Stefan. 'A nice noisy dinner party is always a good idea, especially when one has had a shock. We'll kill a pig!' 'And we'll order an ice-cream cake,' said Magda, 'with all their names on it!' 'And ours too,' said Stefan. 'Certainly!' said Magda. 'Ours too!'

'My very best wishes,' said Miss Cartright. 'May I wish you both every happiness,' said Mr Ryder. Fay smiled ecstatically. She held out her left hand for the customary inspection. 'Lovely,' said Miss Cartright. 'A sapphire. Lovely!' 'A very handsome sparkler,' said Mr Ryder. 'Well I never,' said Miss Jacobs. A whirlwind courtship, with a Hungarian. I never! I hope you'll both be very happy.' Lisa looked at the ring and at Fay. How perfectly astounding it all was. Even she had known Rudi longer than Fay had. How mysterious adult life was after all: she was not now sure that she could have understood what it might all really be about. That Rudi and Fay were now so suddenly engaged to be married – well, it was an event whose preceding stages she could not even guess at. To ascribe the whole process to the operation of love explained nothing. Here however it was, and Fay certainly looked divinely happy.

It was Thursday, which was pay-day, and the announcement had been in the personal column of the morning paper where it had been spotted by Mrs Miles at the breakfast table. 'Fay Baines,' she said. 'Don't you work with a Fay Baines, Lisa?' She was getting quite good now at saying Lisa instead of Lesley. Lisa was so startled at the idea of Rudi and Fay being an engaged couple that she forgot to take the contents of her money box with her, and would have to take delivery of Lisette on the following day. On Thursday night she came home with her pay-packet and taking out her money box she sat on her bed and counted all her money. She counted out exactly £36.15.0 and put it in an envelope. Tomorrow Lisette would be hers.

On Friday morning Fay waylaid her in the Staff Locker Room. 'Oh, Lisa, I've got something here for you from Rudi,' she said. 'From Rudi?' asked the astonished girl. 'Yes, he asked me to apologise for not congratulating you sooner on your results,' said Fay, 'but he said he hoped you'd understand and forgive him in the circumstances. We'll see you on Saturday night at Magda's, won't we? He asked me to give you this, to celebrate your results.' She handed Lisa a package which Lisa opened immediately. It was a large box of expensive chocolates tied with pink ribbon. Lisa gasped. 'Oh, please thank him for me. No one's *ever* given me chocolates before! They're beautiful! Would you like one?' 'No, that's all right,' said Fay. 'It's a bit early in the day for me.' They both laughed. 'It's awfully nice of him,' said Lisa, 'I never expected it, it's awfully nice.' 'Yes, he is nice,' said Fay, 'awfully nice. He really is. He's the nicest man I've ever met.' She smiled happily, and then quite shyly. 'Oh, that's good,' said Lisa. 'I'm very happy for you both, I really am.' 'Thank you,' said Fay. 'Well, I suppose we'd better get ourselves down to Ladies' Cocktail.' 'My second last morning,' said Lisa. 'My thirty-second last, or something,' said Fay. They both laughed. 'The end of an era,' said Lisa. 'Yes,' said Fay, 'it really is. I wonder what's happened to Patty Williams?'

'Perhaps she's pregnant,' said Lisa, 'don't you think?' 'Gee, that's an idea,' said Fay. 'She's certainly waited long enough.' She hoped she wouldn't have to wait as long. She didn't for a moment seriously imagine that she would.

Miss Cartright was leaving half an hour early because she had to go to the dentist. She saw Mr Ryder on her way out. 'Such goings on,' she said. 'I suppose you've noticed we're losing half of Ladies' Cocktail. Miss Baines has given us one month's notice – *not* a long engagement! And I have a funny feeling that we won't be seeing much more of Mrs Williams. I don't know why.' 'Oh well,' said Mr Ryder, 'change is the law of life, my dear.' 'Still,' said Miss Cartright, 'I'd better speak to Personnel tomorrow. We need one more permanent staff member immediately and a possible other soon.' Mr Ryder surveyed his territory. Trade! It was a wonderful spectacle. All of human life is here, he thought. They come and they go. One thing only remains constant, and that's Miss Jacobs – the dear. How I wonder – well, there you are.

He was feeling entirely philosophical by five-thirty; he got ready to leave and walked slowly down the fire stairs. A few dawdlers hurried past him; the building was now virtually empty and in a minute would be closed, locked and bolted fast against the night. He thought he might walk along Elizabeth Street this evening; it was more peaceful. As he approached King Street he noticed a familiar slim figure some distance ahead of him. Ah, he said to himself, there's young Lisa. How she'd grown up in the six or seven weeks she'd been with them: she'd been a child, frail, skinny; now she was a slim young lady with a string of exam results. He watched her walking along ahead, quite self-possessed, quite poised. She was carrying a large dress box of the kind they used in Model Gowns, dark blue with a discreet yellow label dead centre on the lid. My, he thought, they learn fast, the young ladies. Five minutes working with Magda and they're buying Model Gowns. Well, more strength to her arm. Must've splashed out her total wages. Back into the business! Under her other arm was another smaller box tied with pink ribbon. Chocolates? Can't think what else it might be. Now then. Young girl. New frock. Box of chocolates. That's all just as it should be!

Madeleine St John

An obituary by Christopher Potter

Madeleine St John wrote four novels in her short writing life. She was fifty-two when the first, *The Women in Black*, was published in 1993. The other three followed soon after, and form a loose trilogy set in contemporary London; Notting Hill, where she lived most of her adult life, particularly favoured. *The Essence of the Thing* (1997) was shortlisted for the Booker Prize. She also left behind an unfinished manuscript.

Language and a questioning faith are the two poles of St John's created world, as may also have been true of her domestic world. In a last letter, to her beloved vicar, Father Alex Hill, she wrote: 'If I have managed to be a Christian at all, it is due to the marvellous Book of Common Prayer.' Beneath the sly and witty veneer of her writing, she explores questions that are basically theological: we must do the right thing, but how can we tell what the right thing is? This question is at the heart of all of her novels.

In 2002 Madeleine St John prepared strict funeral instructions. She was very ill for at least the last decade of her life. Emphysema made her a virtual recluse, though her illness did not stop her smoking. Her tin of Golden Virginia was often to be seen next to her inhaler, and later, her oxygen supply. Her reclusiveness was furthered by the fact that she lived, for the last twenty years of her life, on the top floor of a house owned by the Notting Hill Housing Trust. She called herself a housing trustafarian.

She claimed to be a de facto recluse for lack of money – not that St John ever complained of her lot – but her isolation was not entirely outside her control. St John could be very entertaining company, but she had a habit of casting anyone who got too close into outer darkness, usually for reasons entirely opaque to the one cast out. She could just as easily reel friends back in, and for similarly mysterious reasons. She lived by a strict moral code, the rules of which were only truly clear to herself.

Her strict funeral instructions were ingeniously and subversively carried out by Fr Alex. Though no reference was to be made to her life, Fr Alex managed to circumvent this by speaking of her before the service began, a sly and witty ploy that Madeleine would surely have appreciated.

The control and desire for anonymity were typical St John qualities. At her death, her always Spartan flat was found to have been even further denuded. An obviously brand-new address book contained the telephone numbers of only a handful of people.

Her estranged sister, Collette, has written that St John's writing emerged out of a life full of an 'enormous amount of pain and suffering'. Madeleine St John was born in 1941 in a smart suburb of Sydney called Castlecrag. Her father, Edward St John, was the son of a Church of England canon and a descendant of many famous St Johns, including Ambrose St John, who converted to Rome and was a close friend of Cardinal John Henry Newman, and Oliver St John, who challenged the legality of Charles I's so-called ship money.

Edward St John, too, challenged unfairness where he found it. As a distinguished QC and a renegade Liberal MP, he spoke out against apartheid and nuclear armament. He almost single-handedly undermined John Gorton, drawing attention in the House to the Prime Minister's rackety private life; he later resigned. Edward was said to be a cold and distant father, though Madeleine admitted that he had given her a lot, including a love of literature. But the relationship deteriorated. The rift grew and the estrangement became permanent. Edward St John died in 1994.

Madeleine's adored mother, Sylvette, was born in Paris. Sylvette's parents were Romanian Jews – Jean and Feiga Cargher – who arrived in Paris in 1915 and fled for Australia in 1934. At first, Sylvette and Edward were happily married, but the marriage turned sour. Sylvette was a depressive and committed suicide in 1954 when Madeleine was twelve.

At the instruction of their father, Madeleine and her younger sister had been sent to a private school that Madeleine likened to Lowood. It was there that the news of their mother's death was broken to them by the headmistress, who told them that they were never to speak of their mother again. Madeleine never referred to this event in public, observing only that the death of her mother 'obviously changed everything'. Edward St John remarried. There were three sons from the second marriage.

Madeleine read English at Sydney University, graduating in 1963, the year, according to Philip Larkin, that 'sex began'. In Sydney, 1963 was the year the satirical magazine *Oz* was first published. Its editor, Richard Walsh, was a contemporary from university. Perhaps coincidentally, Edward St John was to defend him at the first *Oz* obscenity trial in 1964.

Other contemporaries from that remarkable year at Sydney University included Germaine Greer, Clive James, the film director

Bruce Beresford, the poet Les Murray, the historian Robert Hughes, and John Bell, Australia's foremost Shakespearean actor. It was at the university dramatic society that Beresford first met St John. (He is her literary executor.) 'I remember being very struck by her verbal ripostes and observations about our associates.'

Honi Soit, the student paper, described her performance as the whip-cracking courtesan Lola Montez as a 'roly-poly barrel of fun', a description that would amaze anyone who only knew the older St John, but, as a friend of hers recently observed, 'You should have seen her when she was young.'

For all her wit and brilliance – Richard Walsh remembers her as the first person he knew who had read Proust – St John had few close friends at university. She said later that she had the 'somewhat laughable idea that university was a place where nothing happened but a devotion to the truth and an attempt to understand it'. She was unusual amongst that libertarian society for being an avid churchgoer, a lifelong habit, and for having a famous father.

Soon after graduating, St John married a fellow student, Christopher Tillam, who became a filmmaker. They lived in California briefly, before she went on ahead to England, where her husband was to join her. He never arrived and divorce followed. St John never remarried.

As an outsider, St John was fascinated by the English. She said that England 'was everything one had hoped for and has continued to be so':

'I was brought up on the idea that England was where I came from, in a deep sense where I belonged. Australia was a deviation of one's essence.'

Though she never had much money, she found the pre-Thatcher years suited her well enough:

'I had a succession of little jobs in bookshops and offices. There were plenty of jobs if you got bored.'

But the jobs eventually dried up – except for a couple of days a week working in an antique shop in Church Street, Kensington – and St John realised that her CV 'looked like a nightmare'. She spent the next eight years attempting to write a biography of Madame Blavatsky, a manuscript she ultimately destroyed.

Her first novel came more easily. She wrote it, in long hand, in six months. *The Women in Black* is a perfect-pitch comedy of manners set in the ladies' cocktail section of F.G. Goode's, a department store in 1950s Sydney. Though St John claimed she could never 'pull off' anything autobiographical, it is hard not to see some of her in the protagonist Lesley Miles, the clever girl ('"A clever girl is the most wonderful thing in all Creation", said Miss Jacobs') hoping to go up to university, and who changes her name to Lisa.

A Pure Clear Light followed in 1996 and *A Stairway to Paradise* in 1999. But her third novel, *The Essence of the Thing*, probably her masterwork: 'a further chapter', as one of the characters remarks, 'in the gruesome, yet frequently hilarious saga of the island people who had given the planet its common language and virtually all its games'.

Christopher Potter, 2006

I had a succession of little jobs in bookshops and offices. There were plenty of jobs if you were bored.'

But the jobs eventually dried up – except for a couple of days a week working in an antiques shop in Church Street, Kensington – and St John realised that her CV looked like a nightmare. She spent the next eight years attempting to write a biography of Madame Blavatsky, a manuscript she ultimately destroyed.

Her first novel came more easily. She wrote it, in longhand, in six months. *The Women in Black* is a perfect-pitch comedy of manners set in the ladies' cocktail section of F.W. Goode's department store in 1950s Sydney. Though St John claimed she could never 'pull off' anything autobiographical, it is hard not to see some of her in the protagonist Lesley Miles, the clever girl ("A clever girl is the most wonderful thing in all Creation," said Miss Jacobs) hoping to go to university and who changes her name to Lisa.

A Pure Clear Light followed in 1996 and *A Stairway to Paradise* in 1999. But her third novel, *The Essence of the Thing*, probably her masterwork, in another chapter, as one of the characters remarks, 'in the gruesome, yet frequently hilarious saga of the island people who had given the planet its common language and virtually all its games'.

Christopher Hart, 2006

CITY OF VEILS

Zoe Ferraris

'Competition to Stieg Larsson from an unexpected quarter'
Sunday Times

The Victim
One scalding afternoon, the mutilated body of a young woman, half naked beneath her burqa, is discovered on a Saudi beach; soon afterwards a Western woman's husband vanishes without trace.

The Place
Jeddah, Saudi Arabia, the City of Veils. A city of narrow streets and closed shutters, where nothing is what it seems; and the Empty Quarter – one of the most beautiful, yet unforgiving deserts on earth.

The People
Miriam Walker, alone in an alien culture, desperate to find her missing husband. Katya, a forensic scientist battling the prejudices of a society full of sexual, religious and moral contradictions; and Nayir, devout Muslim, desert guide, amateur sleuth – the man she loves.

ABACUS
978-0-349-12213-7

OLD FILTH

Jane Gardam

'A masterpiece'
Guardian

FILTH, in his heyday, was an international lawyer with a practice in the Far East. Now, only the oldest QCs and Silks can remember that his nickname stood for Failed In London Try Hong Kong.

Long ago, Old Filth was a Raj orphan – one of the many young children sent 'Home' from the East to be fostered and educated in England. *Old Filth* tells his story, from his birth in what was then Malaya to the extremities of his old age. In so doing, Jane Gardam not only encapsulates a whole period from the glory days of the British Empire, through the Second World War, to the present and beyond, but also illuminates the complexities of the character known variously as Eddie, the Judge, Fevvers, Filth, Master of the Inner Temple, Teddy and Sir Edward Feathers.

ABACUS
978-0-349-11840-6

THE MAN IN THE WOODEN HAT

Jane Gardam

'What a lot Jane Gardam knows about love and its accommodations; the rich contradictory play of desire and loyalty; the sudden storms of feeling. And how elegantly and intelligently she writes about the instinctive, tendril-like gropings of one human heart towards another'
Jane Shilling, *Daily Telegraph*

Old Filth told the story of Sir Edward (Eddie) Feathers QC, aka Filth – his colonial upbringing and career, his long and comfortable marriage, his rivalries and friendships. *The Man in the Wooden Hat* picks up these threads from the perspective of Filth's wife, Betty. An orphan of the Japanese internment camps, a free spirit, a clever code-breaker at Bletchley Park, Betty has her own secret passions. No wonder she is drawn to Filth's hated rival at the Bar, the brash, forceful Veneering.

ABACUS
978-0-349-11846-8